ESKER

D. L. TRACEY

authorHOUSE®

AuthorHouse™
1663 Liberty Drive
Bloomington, IN 47403
www.authorhouse.com
Phone: 1 (800) 839-8640

Published by AuthorHouse 12/13/2016

ISBN: 978-1-5246-5466-5 (sc)
ISBN: 978-1-5246-5464-1 (hc)
ISBN: 978-1-5246-5465-8 (e)

Library of Congress Control Number: 2016920631

Print information available on the last page.

Any people depicted in stock imagery provided by Thinkstock are models, and such images are being used for illustrative purposes only.
Certain stock imagery © Thinkstock.

This book is printed on acid-free paper.

This book is dedicated to
My Lost Flowers

Devlin & Gabrielle

CONTENTS

PROLOGUE

THE LAST GLACIAL PERIOD, popularly known as the Ice Age, was the most recent glacial period within the current ice age, occurring during the last years of the Pleistocene period. This period lasted from approximately 110,000 to 12,000 years ago. Scientists consider this "ice age" to be merely the latest glaciations event in a much larger ice age; one that dates back over two million years and has seen multiple glaciations.

One of these continental glaciers moved on a slow, murderous path down from what now is known as Canada, destroying and consuming everything in its path. Moving down through what would later be called *"the Americas,"* this glacier came to a rest in what is now called Weymouth, Massachusetts. This glacial journey took approximately 100,000 years to complete its 1,000-mile journey to the shores of Weymouth. Add another 10,000 years for the glacier to melt leaving the Esker.

In the 1940's, the Army Corps of Engineers built a small service road atop of the mighty Esker. The service road of tar and gravel stretched the length of the six-mile Esker and to the highest point of 90 feet. The Army Corps of Engineers then dug several miles of massive drainage tunnels under the Esker to help with flooding and drainage problems of a small, growing town called Weymouth.

…And so our story begins - DL Tracey

1964

"GO ON TOMMY, YOU can do it. Go on," the older boy, Scott, yelled in an almost mocking, more like a bullying tone, as he gave the smaller child a rough push on the back to move the smaller child forward towards the darkness.

Eight-year-old Tommy McGrath bent over and peered into the darkness of the massive storm drain pipe that ran under the Esker. A blast of warm summer air flowed softly through the dark drain pipe. The smell of freshly cut grass from Julia Road Park on the other side of the Esker drifted through on the early morning July breeze.

"No, I better not" Tommy said quietly, looking into the massive storm drain. All freckles and bright red hair, the young boy had seen more than his share of visits to the emergency room at the local hospital. Known as a risk taker, Tommy McGrath, of Irish descent, bright red stringy hair that had been chopped short by his father who only knew how to give crew cuts, pale white skin like his mother, and all skin and bones like his dad, had yet to figure out gravity, and took most dares that came the young boy's way. With two broken arms and one broken leg, more cuts, scrapes, and bruises than his parents could count in his young life; the young boy had yet to win many dares.

"I better not," the 8 year-old nervously said again as he peered into the darkness of the storm drain, "My mom will kill me for sure this time if I did this."

Gazing further into the drain, the 8 year-old boy could see what he thought was sun-light piercing the darkness, signaling the end of the storm drain. The drain ran under Esker State Park, and opened into Julia Road Park on the other side of the glacier.

"It'll be wicked easy to do Tommy. We won't tell your mom either, promise. I'll give you two whole dollars if you do it," the older boy Scott said again, as he pushed Tommy towards the drain, a bit rougher this time.

Nine-year-old Steve Weeks chimed in, "How hard can it be? One end to the other and two bucks just for going where we are going anyways."

"Easy money," the older boy Steve repeated again.

"Really, two whole dollars?" Tommy anxiously replied.

"Yes, just make it to the other end. That is all you have to do and the $2 is yours." Holding up $2, the older boy Scott waved the money in Tommy's face.

Two dollars would buy me eight packs of baseball cards little Tommy thought to himself. *Yes, eight packs and I would get a Yaz card for sure and complete my prized Red Sox baseball card collection. Yes, $2, eight packs of baseball cards. I can do this* the young boy thought to himself.

"Go for it Tommy, $2 is easy money for this," the older boy Steve yelled again. Stepping forward, the older boys crowded the smaller boy towards the darkness by cutting off the younger boy's escape. Another shoved him towards the concrete storm drain by the older boy. Scott left little doubt that Tommy was going into the drain.

The three other young boys picked up the dare. "Do it Tommy. Do it. It's easy money, just for a little walk in the dark to the other side of the park."

The older Steve again pushed the smaller boy towards the dark opening.

"You better pay up on the other side Scott," Tommy yelled out as he stooped down to enter the drain tunnel. "I want $2 when I come out on the other side," 8-year-old Tommy McGrath yelled out, as he knew he had to take the dare now.

Turning back towards the drain pipe, the young boy started towards the faint light that signaled the other end of the storm drain. The smell of the cold salt marsh water was everywhere inside the drain pipe, quickly soaking his new sneakers and making it difficult to see as Tommy's eyes began to itch. Water from the top of the concrete pipe ran down his cheeks. Reaching out to steady himself on the cold concrete walls Tommy started to move forward, quickly disappearing into the darkness of the massive storm drain.

"Billy, you stay here in case he comes back and chickens out," the older boy Scott commanded as he pushed Billy towards the storm drain.

Bending over, the younger boy Billy looked into the drain. "I can't even see him anymore," Billy yelled out.

"Keep looking to make sure he doesn't come back. If he does starts coming back, throw rocks at him so he has to go through the drain," Scott yelled out as he and the other two boys started climbing the steep rocky incline over the Esker to the other side, where the drainage pipe came out in the Julia Road Park.

Reaching the top of the Esker, the three boys stopped to catch their breath on the gravel fire road that ran the top of the Esker. The three-minute climb over rocks and sliding gravel had worn the boys out, and they were each grasping for breath. The older boy Steve yelled back down the Esker to Billy, who was still standing guard at the entrance of the storm drain. "Did he come back?"

"No, and I can't see him anymore. He must be almost there," Billy yelled back.

Still gasping for breath Steve yelled again. "Are you sure, Billy?"

Taking one last look into the storm drain, Billy yelled again "Yes, I'm sure; he didn't come back."

Turning towards the rocky path up the Esker, Billy started to climb the steep rocky slope to join his friends on the top. Reaching the top of the Esker, Billy hunched over to catch his breath.

"You sure he didn't come back," the big boy Steve questions the younger boy.

"Ya, I'm sure; I watched the whole time and he did not come back."

"Tommy was going quickly," the younger boy said again, looking towards Julia Road Park on the other side of the Esker to where the pipe exited the side of the mountain in a small ravine at the far edge of centerfield of the ballpark. "I bet he is already there on the other side waiting for his $2," the younger boy Billy blurted out as he continued to catch his breath after the quick climb up the Esker.

"OK, let's go. I want to see him come out of the drain pipe or no $2," the bigger boy Steve yelled as he started to slide down the other side of the Esker.

Rocks and dirt tumbled with the boys as they started their sliding climb down to Julia Road Park that was on the other side of the 12,000-year-old glacier. The storm drain pipe exited from the glacier into a small streambed about 10 feet down in a steep rocky ravine, about 30 feet from the glacier itself. In order to see into the pipe, the young boys needed to climb down the small ravine and come back to the pipe to look into the darkness. The cold smell of the marsh was overwhelming and the boys' feet sank up to their ankles in the gooey salt marsh mud as they started to yell out the boy's name into the darkness.

"Tommy, Tommy you in there?" the young boys yelled together.

"He went back, I bet," the bigger boy Steve said, turning to look at the top of the Esker. "He is not getting my $2," the boy said to the others.

"I saw him go in, Steve," the boy Billy said again. "And he did not come back. Maybe he already made it out and went home."

"No, he was not that fast; and besides, he would have waited for his $2," Steve blurted out.

"Tommy, come on out. We need to get home," Billy yelled into the drain again.

"Ya, Tommy let's go or you don't get the $2," the older boy Steve chimed in.

"Is Tommy in the drain pipe?" A woman's voice yelled down to the four boys.

Turning, the four boys looked up from the ravine and there was Tommy's mother, Mrs. McGrath.

"We told him not to do it Mrs. McGrath," the older boy Steven yelled back. "We told him it was too dangerous to climb through the pipes, but he did it anyways."

The look of panic now covered the older boy's face.

"Tommy is in that drainpipe?" the panicky mother yelled, starting to climb down into the ravine.

"Yes, we think so," the older boy said, looking back into the dark drain as if the young boy would pop out like some sort of magic trick. "Tommy may have already made it out and went home," the older boy said, trying to keep away from the frantic mother as she bent down and looked into the pipe.

"He would not go home, Steve. He would wait for his money," one of the younger boys blurted out.

"What?" the woman asked, turning towards the younger boy.

"Ya. Steve bet Tommy $2 he would not climb through the pipes to this side from the other side," the little boy said as he pointed to the top of the Esker.

"You bet my son to do this Steven?" the mother screeched at the older boy.

"I didn't make him do it. He wanted to," the older boy said as he started to climb out of the ravine.

"Wait till I tell your mother Steven," the woman called out to the older boy as he began to run as if leaving would make it all like it never happened.

Turning back towards the pipe, the woman started to call out her son's name, "Tommy? Tommy?"

"Is everything all right Ruth?"

Turning towards the top of the ravine, the woman saw Bob Crosby, a neighbor who lived across the street from the park.

"The kids say Tommy is climbing though this pipe from the other side of the Esker," the woman said as she yelled her son's name again. "Tommy? Tommy, are you in there?"

"Maybe he did not really do it," the man called down into the ravine.

Before the woman could answer, the chilling scream of a child echoed from the pipe; it was her child.

"Tommy! Tommy!" the woman screamed again. Turning towards the man, the woman yelled, "Bob get help quickly!"

Turning back toward the pipe, the woman continued to yell her son's name as the screams continued.

Turning quickly, Bob Crosby ran towards his home to call the police.

"Car 12, what is your location?" the dispatch voice crackled over the car radio.

Reaching down and grabbing the radio mike, Sergeant Nick Giannone of the Weymouth Police Department looked out the police car window to see the cross street the car had just passed.

"Dispatch, car 12 on Green and passing Sunrise Drive."

"Roger. See the woman at Julia Road Park. Missing child," came the reply from the female dispatch operator.

"Got it. Julia Road Park. Lost child." Hanging up the mike, Sergeant Giannone turned toward his rookie partner, Eddie Hammond, who was looking forward with great anticipation to this first call of his young police officer career.

"Easy, rookie. It's just a lost kid. Heck, he probably already found his way home." Turning the police cruiser onto Julia Road, Officer Giannone gave the car a bit more gas and headed to the park, about 600 yards down the road.

Turning into the park, Officer Giannone could see a group of people gathered out at the far edge of centerfield of the baseball diamond, close to the Esker and the storm drain that ran under the glacier. *Home run territory,* the officer thought as he slowly drove the police cruiser to the franticly waving crowd.

"So much for a lost child," the rookie said as they pulled up to the crowd.

"Look, rookie, we do not jump to conclusions in this business. Let's stick to the facts, find the child, and make it a nice day. However, yes, something is going on here."

Picking up the call mike, the sergeant called out, "Dispatch, car 12. We need a fire rescue team here at Julia Road Park. Possible child trapped in storm drain."

"Roger, fire rescue unit to Julia Road Park. Possible child trapped in storm drain," came the crisp reply of the female dispatcher.

Opening his car door, Officer Giannone climbed out of the police cruiser and walked towards the ever-growing group of kids and adults.

"Officer, my child is lost in those pipes!" the woman screamed franticly, pointing towards the storm drain. Officer Giannone knew this woman. McGrath was her name. She and her family lived two streets over from his home. North Weymouth was not that big of a town, and most folks knew each other to some degree. Next to her were her other two sons Rickey, about 9 years of age, and Glenn, about 5 or so. Both of the kids were feeding off their mother's fear.

"I heard my child screaming in there!" The frantic mother pointed at the storm drain as if the officer was not sure what she was talking about.

"Ricky, right?" Officer Giannone asked as he knelt down in front of the young boy.

"Yes sir," the older son said looking at the officer.

"Good. I need you to take your brother, go home, and see if Tommy is there."

"But mom says Tommy is in there," the boy replied, as he pointed towards the pipe.

"Yes, son, I know what your mother said, but just in case, let's cover all the bases; that is just good police work." Smiling down at the older child, the officer continued, and, "If he is there, come right back and tell me. If not, wait until your mother comes home and tells you what is going on." Turning the boys away from the crowd, the officer gave them a slight push. "Now off with you," the officer growled at the two boys. Turning back towards the drain pipe, the officer turned on his flashlight and started towards the drain opening.

Stooping down to look into the storm drain, the officer flashed his powerful light deep into the pitch-black drain. The cold smell of the salt mash filled the musty drain and the constant dripping of water could be heard coming from the darkened depths.

"Tommy! Tommy!" Officer Giannone yelled. His echo could be heard bouncing around the storm drain. Yelling again, "Tommy! Tommy, this is Officer Giannone. Are you in there?" Turning back towards the mother, the officer asked, "You are sure he is in there?"

But before the mother could reply, a child's voice screamed out in pain and fear from deep in the storm drain's bowels…

"Tommy!" The frantic mother screamed out in fear, lunging towards the storm drain.

Grabbing hold of the terrified mother, Officer Giannone screamed, "Rookie! Get down here!" Jumping down into the drainage ditch, the rookie grabbed hold of the screaming mother.

"Rookie, listen and listen good. Get her out of the drain and get right back down here."

"Right, Sergeant," the rookie yelled as he led the frantic mother to the safety of the ravine ledge and the crowd that was growing by the moment. "Somebody hold this woman and make sure she does not come back down!" the rookie yelled as he headed back into the ravine and to the opening of the storm drain.

"All right rookie, hold my gun and hat. I will be right back," the senior police officer yelled as he handed his gun and hat to the young police officer. "Keep the crowd back and do not let anyone follow me into the drain. That includes you. Understand?" the sergeant yelled.

Dropping to his hands and knees, Officer Giannone quickly started to crawl into the darkness of the storm drain, his light making barely a dent in the darkness in front of him. About 15 feet into the storm drain, the officer came to a hub of pipes; the storm drain split into three other directions besides the outlet he had just entered. He decided to enter the drain on his left, as it seemed to be the logical choice, as it pointed towards the marsh on the other side of the Esker.

"Tommy, Tommy!" the officer called out as he slowed his crawl forward. Sea gulls screaming out their cries echoed into the storm drain from the ocean beyond. The smell of the salty marsh coming from the other end of the storm drain was overwhelming, and the dripping of the salt water on his face and head from the pipe was getting in his eyes, stinging them as he squinted to see ahead of him. Calling out again, "Tommy, Tommy, it is Officer Giannone, where are you?"

For a moment, there was nothing but silence. Then the sound of a whimpering child in great pain and fear came softly echoing ever so slightly off the storm drain's cement walls. He turned his light in the direction of the sound. About 30 feet down the drain, the child's sneakers came slowly into view. Moving a bit forward the office now saw the bottoms of the sneakers came into view of the powerful light. The small feet twitched and the steady flow of blood was now seen flowing between the child's legs moving in the small flow of salt water down the drain towards the officer.

"I found him!" the officer yelled out behind him. "I found him!" the officer yelled out again, moving forward towards the child.

"Tommy, I am here!" the officer yelled as he moved forward again, flashing his light to show the way. Stopping for a moment the officer flashed his light a bit higher to the top of the boy. "What the *F* is that?" the officer half said to himself and to the situation in front of him.

There was something on top of the child, cutting into his belly with what seemed to look like a seashell. It looked like a pile of seaweed or something. The poor child screamed one more time as whatever it was pulled a part of the boy's stomach out…

Rushing forward, on his hands and knees the officer screamed, "Get off of him you bastard!"

"Sergeant, sergeant? Did you find the child?" the rookie thought he heard the senior officer call out.

"I heard him say he found my child!" the distraught mother yelled down from the ravine.

"I heard him also," one of the children in the growing crowd yelled.

"All right, everyone quiet down so I can hear what is going on!" the rookie yelled at the crowd. Turning back to peer into the pipe, the rookie heard a scream of unbelievable terror coming from the storm drain. That scream was Sergeant Giannone's.

WEYMOUTH FIRE STATION ONE

WHAT A MORNING IT had been. Sitting in his office at Weymouth Fire Station One, Captain Butch Hunt contemplated the day at hand. A hot cup of java released its sweet smell of freshly ground Colombian beans into the early morning air. A morning talk show played softly in the corner of the office on a small radio. The morning weather report called for rain later that day and the Red Sox have a game tonight against the Yankees. The announcer yelled "Go Sox!"

"Well, I'd best watch that game tonight; should be a good one," Captain Hunt said aloud, taking a long swig of the hot java. "Yes, a good game indeed."

"Captain, we have a call."

Turning to the voice, the captain saw the station dispatcher standing at the door. Hitting the call bell for the station and jumping to his feet, the captain headed towards the main bay of the fire station as the alarm bell started to ring out through the station in a loud clanking sound.

That bell could wake the dead, the captain thought as he headed in to the dispatcher's station to get the information on the call.

Upstairs at the station, the crew of five was already headed for the famous fire pole to slide down to the first floor where the fire trucks were located.

Hitting the floor first was the newbie driver Paul Tobin. This was a special day for the firefighter, as he had just finished his driving certification, and today was to be his first day behind the wheel of the huge Mack fire truck. Pulling his fire boots on, the young man quickly put on his jacket and helmet; he walked quickly to hit the button to lift the fire station's door, so the Mack fire truck could get loose on the streets of Weymouth.

Climbing into the front of the fire truck, firefighter Tobin hit the igniters and the powerful diesel engine roared to life.

Looking into the side mirrors, the driver could see the other four members of the crew were already climbing on board.

"Where is the captain?" the newbie yelled out the window.

"Right here, kid," Captain Hunt yelled as he climbed up into the cab of the massive truck. "OK, Julia Road Park," the captain yelled above the roar of the diesel. "We have a missing or trapped child in one of the storm drains."

"Right, sir," the nervous truck driver replied. "Julia Road Park."

"Easy, kid. I'm sure the child is already at home and this is just an exercise for us today."

Looking out the window, Captain Hunt could see the skies already turning a dark gray with rain clouds. If that happened, this rescue could get dicey quick, as every storm drain in Weymouth emptied into the Esker at some point right.

Ah, the kid is probably already home. Captain Hunt thought. Hitting the siren and lights, Captain Hunt yelled, "Roll it, Tobin."

Hitting the accelerator, the mighty Mack truck leapt out of the station garage. Turning onto North Street, Captain Hunt pulled the rope that controlled the air horn on top of the truck. The ear-splitting horn screamed out in pain, warning anyone near that the fire truck was turning onto the main road.

"OK Paul, down to Shaw, and take a left," the captain called out.

"Right, sir," came the excited call back from the driver.

At that moment, the call radio blared into life. *"Officer down! Officer down!"* came the frantic call over the radio.

"Say again," was the dispatcher's response.

"This is Officer Hammond. Officer down! Sergeant Giannone heard the child screaming in the drain and went in after him. A few minutes later, I heard Sergeant Giannone screaming and then all went quiet. I kept calling, but he does not respond."

Again, the frantic voice called over the radio. "Officer down! Officer down!"

"Roger. Officer down help is on the way," came the cool reply of the female dispatcher.

Picking up the call mike, Captain Hunt called out, "Dispatch, Engine One responding to scene. Please send another fire unit and dispatch an ambulance to scene."

"Confirm," came the dispatcher's reply. "One additional unit and an ambulance are being dispatched to scene."

Turning onto Shaw Street, the air horn sounded again almost shutting out the sound of the screaming siren. Looking past, the newbie driver and out the side window, Captain Hunt could see a group of children looking at the racing fire truck from the windows of the public library.

"Spring break this week, Mr. Tobin. Let's keep a sharp eye out for kids in the street," Captain Hunt yelled above the roar of the Mack diesel, pulling the air horn again to make the point.

Racing down Shaw Street, the captain could hear the wail of police units starting to respond off in the distance.

"OK, Mr. Tobin. Let's slow down; we have a stop sign coming up at the bottom of Shaw."

"Yes sir, I know," said the driver. *Heck, I grew up right around here,* the cadet thought, but dared not speak it out loud, as Captain Hunt was not much for chit chat when it came to a mission.

Slowing the mighty fire truck down was no easy task as the driver started to bring it to a slow walk through the intersection. The captain again laid on the horn to announce the presence of the fire truck moving through the cross streets. Hitting the gas again, the Mack leapt forward as the captain yelled above the roar, "OK, get ready; we have a big turn onto Green just up ahead."

At that moment, a police interceptor cruiser flew by the rapidly accelerating fire truck, lights and siren blaring towards Green Street. Slowing down, the police cruiser came to a halt in the middle of the street, stopping traffic both ways for the fire truck.

"He is stopping traffic, Captain," the driver called out over the roar of the sirens.

"Follow procedure, Mr. Tobin," came the curt reply from Captain Hunt.

Bringing the fire tuck to a slow halt, the driver looked both ways on Green and started to move forward again. Captain Hunt again pulled on the rope as the horn blared the arrival of the truck at the intersection and they moved forward. The fire truck again began gaining speed as the police cruiser flew by the slower moving truck again like the fire truck was moving backwards, heading towards the next intersection that led to Julia Road.

"OK, Mr. Tobin, this is where it gets tricky," Captain Hunt, yelled above the roar of the sirens.

The intersection was a four-way turn with Elvia Road coming down off a steep hill and Julia Road on the other side connected by a sharp turn, all downhill to Green Street.

"At least there is no traffic," Captain Hunt yelled out, this mainly due to the fact that two Weymouth police cruisers now blocked both sides of the intersection allowing the fire truck to cross at a slow clip. Sounding the horn one last time, Captain Hunt shut down the sirens as they were now in a heavily populated residential area and close to Julia Road Park.

"We do not need any children running out to see what is going on. Slow it down, Mr. Tobin," the captain called out. "Six hundred yards and we are there."

Looking down Julia Road, the captain could see two police cruisers already on scene as one of the cruisers again whipped past the fire truck heading up Frank Road to come into the park from the other side.

While the massive fire truck pulled into the park, the captain could see a few problems already mainly because of the crowd. It appeared that 50 or so people were gathered around something in deep centerfield of the ballpark. Because his kids played ball here, the captain knew where the storm drain was. After all, it was a "ball gobbler" for sure. How many baseballs had fallen into that ravine? An automatic double was the rule if the ball dropped into that ravine.

"Mr. Tobin, pull to the left of the crowd and power down."

Picking up the radio mike, Captain Hunt called out "Engine One on scene."

"Roger. Engine one on scene. Engine two in route. Estimated time to arrival two minutes," came the reply of the female dispatcher.

Good. That is Captain Hill and his squad. I am going to need another veteran team for this, I bet the Captain thought.

As he started to climb out of the fire truck, he noticed the first drops of rain beginning to splat on the fire truck's windshield, and the sound of thunder echoed off in the distance of the graying sky.

"We better hurry this one, men," Captain Hunt yelled as he jumped to the ground from the fire truck and started toward the growing crowd of onlookers.

SEARCH AND RESCUE

"**M**Y SON IS TRAPPED somewhere in the storm drains!" the frantic mother yelled at Captain Hunt as the firefighter approached the crowd of 30 to 40 on lookers now, and growing at a rapid pace.

"Yes, ma'am, now please step back and let us go to work," Captain Hunt responded, barely missing a step as he headed towards the ravine. No time for politeness; a child's life, and that of a police officer, hung in the balance. Politeness would have to wait. It was all about time now, with a wicked bad storm approaching. "Sergeant Collins, please get your men to move this crowd back at least 50 feet from the scene," Captain Hunt yelled at the lead police officer on scene.

"We have an officer down here!" the officer screamed back.

Stopping in his tracks, Captain Hunt walked over to the officer and quietly said "Yes, and we have a lost child, or maybe you should go tell that mother that her child will have to wait? Now move this crowd back and let me and my men do our job," the Captain yelled as he turned back towards the ravine.

Climbing down into the ravine followed by Sergeant Collins and three firefighters, Captain Hunt bent down and looked into the darkness of the storm drain. "Give me a torch," (slang used by firefights for flashlight) the captain yelled out, still looking into the drain. Immediately a powerful torch was held over his shoulder, its powerful light barely making a dent into the haze of the saltwater mist and darkness of the storm drain. Taking the torch in hand, the captain crawled in a few feet pushing the light ahead of him.

The icy coldness of the concrete tube could be felt even through the captain's overalls; a steady flow of water was now running through the storm drain. Time would soon be a precious commodity in this search and rescue. Coming to the intersection of the four drains, the captain knew this was not going to be a quick rescue, as the sound of thunder echoed into the drains.

"Damn," he said while flashing the powerful flashlight down each of the drains, the light reflected back from the saltwater haze. "No more than 10 feet visibility at this point," Captain Hunt yelled out. "We're going to have to do this the hard way." Turning around, the firefighter crawled out of the drain as the rain turned into a heavy downpour.

Climbing out of the ravine, the captain noticed the crowd was gone due to the thunder and lightning that filled the sky; just the mother of the lost child was standing by herself next to the fire truck. The rain had already drenched her, and the captain could see the woman shaking. Was it from the cold, or knowing her son was somewhere under the Esker?

"Tobin, get over here!" Captain Hunt yelled out.

"Yes, sir!" the driver yelled above the thunder.

"Get the mother into the fire truck and out of the rain, and then get back here."

"Yes, sir!" yelled the firefighter, as he turned and ran to help the woman into the fire truck.

"Captain Hill, take your crew over the glacier to the storm drain on the other side. Pointing to the top of the glacier, Captain Hunt continued, "Send in one man 50 feet with a torch, tied off, and begin a search and rescue. Be quick about it. These drains will be filling with rain-water pretty quick. We have maybe an hour at best. I will send in one man here 50 feet, tied off also, and let's see what is between them with the lights."

"Can do!" Captain Hill yelled out, against the rain and thunder as lightning filled the sky. "Billy, Jimmy, and Shaun, let's go grab your gear. We are going for a climb."

Turning towards the glacier, Captain Hill and his men headed for the climb over the glacier.

"Make it quick, Phil. This storm is going to fill these drains quickly," Captain Hunt called out again to the men as they began their climb up the glacier.

Turning toward his crew, Captain Hunt quickly said, "Huddle up men. OK, here is the mission: Tobin in the drain with a strong torch, 50 feet in down the left drain and light up the drain with the fire-fighter at the other end. I will follow up on Tobin. James, you rope us off and stay outside the drain. Give us no more than 50 feet of line. Is that understood?" Captain Hunt yelled out above the roar of the thunder and stinging rain.

"Yes, sir!" came the team of firefighters' reply.

"Good! Men, get a move on then, and be quick about it. This rain does not give us much time."

Turning towards the glacier, Captain Hunt saw the other rescue team had made it to the top in spite of the muddy climb, and were now headed down the other side of the steep glacier.

"OK men, let's get this done," Captain Hill yelled out over the roar of the thunder and the driving rain. Reaching the bottom of the glacier, the firefighters gathered around the opening of the storm drain.

The wind howled off the marsh from the Back River. The tall marsh grass played an eerie tune as the wind slapped it around and howled down into the storm drain in a whooshing sound. The rain-water was already flowing out of the storm drain at a rapid clip, and to top it off, high tide had started, so the ocean was starting to back-fill the marsh where the storm drain emptied out.

"OK, Shaun, hook me. I'm going in," Captain Hill yelled above the roar of the crashing thunder. Taking off his fire helmet and jacket, the captain lifted his arms for the fire harness to be attached around his waist.

"Not a good idea, Captain. Let me take this one."

"Not a chance. I need you out here to run the rescue while I get out of the rain. Trust me, Shaun. This is the best way to run this operation."

Grabbing the powerful torch, Captain Hill turned, bent down, and started the slow crawl into the dark storm drain, pushing the powerful touch in front of him.

"Billy, harness up and get after the captain. Try to keep him out of trouble and while you're at it, keep it safe," firefighter Shaun yelled above the storm.

"Already on it, Shaun," the firefighter yelled, dropping to his knees and following Captain Hill into the darkness of the storm drain.

"Ready firefighter?" Captain Hunt yelled as he tightened the harness around the waist of the young firefighter.

"Not really, sir" came the nervous reply from the young firefighter.

Laughing a bit, the captain replied, "Do not blame you one bit," the captain yelled above the storm. "We get in, find the officer and child, and get out, no problem. You will be in sight of me at all times. I will be following you in and keeping you in sight at all times. Do you get that firefighter?" Captain Hunt yelled again above the crack of thunder.

"Yes, sir," came the crisp reply.

"On with ya then before I take the lead." Bending down with the powerful torch in front of him the young firefighter started to crawl into the storm drain followed a few seconds later by the captain.

"Keep moving Paul," Captain Hunt yelled to the young firefighter. "In a few feet you will come to an intersection of the drains; take the left storm drain for 20 feet and then stop," Captain Hunt yelled above the roar of the thunder and the flow of rushing water.

Coming to the intersection, the young firefighter stopped for a moment. *This is crazy,* he thought to himself. There was already a steady flow of water running through the drains and it was getting higher by the moment. Struggling to breathe in the air laden with the salt mist, the young firefighter stopped to get his bearings. The sound of thunder and lightning echoing through the storm drain, with the cold wind whipping off the Atlantic, filled the storm drain with an eerie howling sound. It seemed as if the concrete walls were closing in on the young firefighter. Fighting off claustrophobia, the young firefighter started to focus on the rescue. *OK,* he thought, *we are looking for a police officer and a child. Should not be too hard to find them is this pipe.*

Wiping the mist from his eyes, the rookie was certain something, or someone, was watching him from the drain to his right. Quickly flashing the beam down the right drain, the light was reflected back by the saltwater mist as the sound of flowing water continued from the drain.

"I can't see 10 feet in front of me, Captain," the young firefighter yelled over his shoulder to Captain Hunt, who was now right behind him in the narrow storm drain. The water was now above the wrists of the firefighters as they continued to crawl towards the left drain junction.

A tight pull on his safety harness signaled 50 feet into the storm drain. Wiping the salt mist from his eyes, Captain Hill began the search process with his powerful torch. Flashing the beam in front of him, the powerful light began penetrating the saltwater mist deeper into the massive storm drain.

"I got some movement," Captain Hill yelled out, as something was moving about another 100 feet down the drain.

"What do you got Cap?" Billy yelled as he neared the captain in the storm drain.

"Not sure, really. Still a bit too far to make out for sure".

"Is it the other team?" Billy yelled above the roar of the wind whipping down the drain.

Both of the firefighters were soaked with a wall of salt water that was entering the drain from the marsh. A crack of lightning lit the drain for just a split second as another lightning strike happened just outside the drain.

"*THERE!*" Captain Hill yelled pointing with the torch as lightning lit the storm drain once more.

"I didn't see it, Captain; what was it?" Billy yelled from behind the captain.

"It looked like the police officer on his back, but moving down the drain. Like he was being dragged by something. Captain Hill yelled out above the roar of the wind howling through the drain. "We need to move quickly. We can't wait for Captain Hunt and his team. *GIVE ME MORE ROPE!*" Captain Hill yelled as he quickened his crawl deeper into the dark storm drain.

Moving slowly into the left storm drain, firefighter Tobin began the slow crawl down the narrow concrete drain.

"Man, it is getting cold, Captain," the young firefighter called out over the crashing sound of the lighting as the eerie sound of the cold wind echoed through the storm drains, pushing the incoming Back River tide with it.

"Keep moving; we have another 25 feet to go," Captain Hunt yelled out as he turned to enter the left storm drain. Stopping for a moment, Captain Hunt flashed his light down the drain to his right. "Hold up Paul. I have some movement in the right drain. Back up, firefighter, I need some slack in our harness!" Captain Hunt yelled out as the firefighter started towards the right drain, pushing his flashlight ahead of him.

"I hear ya, Captain", the young firefighter called out, as he started to back up in the narrow drain. "Damn. Not enough room to turn around," firefighter Tobin yelled out as he continued his backward motion into the intersection of the four drains.

"TOMMY? TOMMY?" Captain yelled above the roar of the incoming saltwater and thunder crashing as it echoed through the storm drains.

"Did you find the kid?" firefighter Tobin yelled out as he turned to follow the captain into the next storm drain.

"I think so," Captain Hunt yelled out as he moved forward on his hands and knees to the shadow ahead in the drain. Flashing his powerful torch towards the shadow the child came into view. "Oh dear God," Captain Hunt half said to himself as he started to shake. Was it the cold ocean water that filled the storm drain, or the gruesome scene in front of him?

"CAPTAIN, DID YOU FIND THE KID?" the young firefighter yelled out as he crawled up behind the captain in the narrow storm drain.

"THERE HE IS! MOVE!" Captain Hill yelled out as he saw the police officer about 15 feet ahead of him now. Pushing the powerful torch ahead of him the captain could see that the police officer had stopped moving down the drain. Laying in a fetal position on his left side, there was no sign of life from the police officer. Moving closer, Captain Hill was not sure, but there seemed to be movement just past the body of the officer.

"HUNT? Is that you?" the captain yelled out above the roar of rushing water that was now filling the storm drains at a rapid clip. The cold wind whipping off the Atlantic through the drain pipe was making the rescue an impossible task, spraying the cold salt water as it smashed against the concrete walls of the storm drain. The temperature continued to drop as the water from the cold Atlantic Ocean continued to rush down the drain with the fury of Mother Nature. Damn, what is that movement in the drain? Reaching out, the firefighter grabbed the police officer by the leg and turned him over to get his face out of the rushing salt water.

"CAPTAIN HUNT, DID YOU FIND THE CHILD?" the firefighter asked while grabbing the captain's boot. Firefighter Tobin yelled out again, *"DO YOU HAVE THE KID?"*

Frozen for a moment, the tough Irish firefighter captain silently began to pray, *"Dear God, what have you let happen to this child?"*

At that moment, the wind seemed to die down and the water slowed to an eerie stillness in the storm drain; a slow dripping of water could be heard in the distance as the echo slowly bounced off the drain pipe. The light from the powerful torch illuminated the child who was now mere feet from the captain.

"Dear God," the captain murmured again.

The child sat hunched over in the light. His skin was a dull, ashen gray; the terror still etched on his face from the horror of his own death. The child's body had been cut open it appeared, from neck to his navel. All of his organs seemed to be missing, just an empty bloody shell of what a child used to be. Suddenly, the head of the child looked up and the horror of his death was ever so apparent on the lifeless face, etched forever in the last painful moments of the young child's precious life.

Something had grabbed the hair on the back of the child's head and was quickly dragging the child farther down the drain like a broken doll. Pushing forward, Captain Hunt grabbed the child's leg and tried to stop whatever had the child in its death grasp.

"BASTARD! LET GO OF THIS CHILD!" the captain screamed out, as the water began crashing again and the wind started to howl like the screaming agony of a painful death through the storm drains.

The fight for the lifeless body of the child was on and Captain Hunt was determined to win this fight. Pulling harder on the leg of the child, the firefighter stopped the movement of the child down the drain.

"I HAVE YOU TOMMY!" the firefighter screamed, dragging the child back towards the entrance of the storm drain. *"PULL TOBIN, PULL!"* Captain Hunt screamed, dragging the lifeless body of the child towards the entrance of the massive storm drain.

Turning the police officer over to get his face out of the rushing water, Captain Hill fought the nausea that started to overwhelm him. The police officer's face had been stripped from his head, right to the bone, like the officer had shaved a bit too close and ripped all of his skin off. Something was embedded deeply into the skull where the police officer's nose used to be. Reaching forward, Captain Hill touched the white colored object that was embedded in the officer's face. It was a sea shell of some sort, the captain thought fingering the object. It was almost as if something or someone was using the shell to split open the skull, but the firefighters had interrupted the process.

WHACK! at that moment, something struck the firefighter's helmet with a violent force that almost knocked Captain Hill out. Fighting to regain focus, the firefighter knew he needed to move quickly as another blow hit the firefighter's helmet. Attaching his safety harness to the belt of the police officer, Captain Hill yelled *"PULL!"* over his shoulder and started to crawl backwards the way he had came in a few moments ago. The officer's body quickly started to move as the three men outside the drain started to pull the safety rope in a rapid motion, sensing the urgency in their captain's voice.

Crawling backwards is never an easy task. Crawling backwards in a drain pipe in the midst of a raging storm is damn near impossible. Captain Hill yelled out in pain as his head was hit again by some sort of object coming from the drain in front of him. Blood was now streaming down the firefighter's face, making it difficult to see where the flying objects were coming from. Reaching down into the rising water, the captain found the object that had cut his face open. Jamming the object into his breast pocket, he would have to look at it later, as time was something the firefighter was quickly running out of.

The Atlantic Ocean was nearing high tide as the cold salt water was now rushing into the drain; the freight train noise was deafening as the waves crashed into the opening of the drain now filled marsh and half filling the massive storm drain. The sun had long since been blotted out by the massive storm clouds; and the driving rain made it difficult for the men outside the drain to see anything as they continued to pull the rope that was attached to the safety harness.

"We have something!" one of the firefighters yelled as he started to pull the lifeless body of the police officer from the storm drain. Reaching down, the other two firefighters helped pull the officer from the drain.

"Get him in the stretcher basket now!" Shaun yelled out, grabbing the officer's legs.

Next out of the drain came firefighter Billy, soaking wet and out of breath; he could barely talk. *"THE CAPTAIN! THE CAPTAIN!"* Billy tried to yell out but mostly water came out of the young firefighter's mouth as he pointed back towards the drain. "Something attacked the captain down the drain as we were pulling the cop out. Something attacked the captain," the firefighter repeated again, pointing still at the storm drain.

What the f… is that? Captain Hill thought.

Continuing backing out of the drain, the firefighter saw movement. Something was thrashing towards him and closing fast. It looked like a big ball of seaweed or something. *"FLASH"* a crack of lightning struck outside the massive storm drain, casting an eerie glow down the drain. Whatever was coming towards the firefighter stopped for a moment as the crack of thunder stopped it in its tracks. The eerie glow in the storm drain illuminated the creature for a moment and the firefighter stopped moving in disbelief, not sure what it was.

The creature was covered in seaweed, obscuring its form. At that moment, the creature lifted its head and stared at the firefighter. Large yellow eyes were now glaring at the firefighter. A low snarl started to fill the storm drain and the creature started moving forward slowly at first, almost like knowing it had cornered its prey and was slowly moving in for the kill. Stopping for a moment, the creature started to growl; a slow, deep growl that made the storm drain feel even colder than its concrete walls. Seeing the breath of the creature as it snorted, the firefighter knew it was time to move. Moving backwards, the firefighter heard a loud hideous scream as the creature started forward again, rapidly; and closing the distance in mere seconds. Raising his arms for protection, the firefighter began to scream as the creature was upon him.

"WE HAVE YOU CAPTAIN!" Pulling the fire chief out of the storm drain, the firefighters lifted the captain to his feet.

"Are you OK Captain?" Billy yelled as the roaring wind and driving rain made talk more of a yelling thing right now.

"Ya, I am fine Billy. Give me your torch."

Taking the powerful flashlight, the fire chief bent down and peered into the flowing storm drain. Whatever it was, it had retreated into the darkness of the massive storm drain.

"What was it Capitan?" Billy yelled out. He bent down and looked into the flowing storm drain.

"Don't know for sure, but it was mean."

Reaching into his shirt pocket, the fire chief pulled out the object that the creature had thrown at him. Fingering the white object in his hand, the firefighter turned it over a few times and just said, "Seashell. That damn thing attacked me with seashells. Grab the body; we need to get out of here. This rescue is over. Let's hope Captain Hunt has found the child."

Grabbing the stretcher with the dead officer on it, the firefighters began to climb out of marsh and over the hill to the waiting ambulance on the other side at the park.

"PULL, TOBIN, PULL!" Captain Hunt screamed again. Grasping the child by his ankle, Captain Hunt fought to stay focused as the cold Atlantic Ocean water began to swirl around him in the darkened storm drain. Pushing backwards with his left hand, the captain could feel something grasp the child again and tried to pull the lifeless body farther into the endless darkness of the storm drain.

Grabbing the safety line, firefighter Tobin began to pull. Looking over the shoulder of Captain Hunt, the young firefighter was not sure what was going on; but it appeared the captain did have the child, and something was fighting with the captain for control of the child.

Lunging forward, Captain Hunt began to cover the child with his body. Whatever had attacked this child had come back with a vengeance and wanted the child's body. With salt water stinging his eyes, Captain Hunt began to try and fight back with whatever it was in that storm drain.

Punching out with his left hand, Captain Hunt hit what he thought was seaweed. A sharp pain greeted his punch. Pulling his hand back, the firefighter began to lose consciousness as he realized that most of his had was a mangled mess and was hanging from his arm held on only by some tissue. Moving forward, the firefighter tried to place his body in front of the child and continue to protect the lifeless body, but that was the last thing the captain remembered as he felt a sharp pain to his head as he blacked out.

Moving backwards in the rising water, the young firefighter could feel the resistance of his pulling as the captain's body had gone limp. Yelling over his shoulder and tugging his safety line, the firefighter yelled *"PULL US OUT!"* he yelled again *"PULL US OUT!"*

The Atlantic Ocean was rushing into the storm drain like a freight train. They had stayed to long and now the likelihood of getting out was grim at best. Grabbing the captain's safety line, the young firefighter pulled harder. This time the captain's body began to move backwards. Thank God. The crew outside must have heard his screams as the safety line began a rapid pull towards the entrance of the storm drain.

Fighting to keep his head above the raging water, the young firefighter continued to pull Captain Hunt with him. Popping into the intersection of pipes, the young firefighter fell backwards losing his torch. The storm drain went black. At this point Captain Hunt came flowing out of the storm drain into the connector drain. Grabbing the collar of the captain's shirt, the young firefighter yelled again. *"PULL! PULL!"* A sharp pull on the harness came from the crew outside the drain, and the last few feet was under water as the drain entrance was now covered with water that was flowing into the ravine.

Out popped firefighter Tobin. Struggling to stand, he yelled, *"HELP! THE CAPTAIN HAS BEEN HURT!"*

Pulling with what was left of his strength, the young firefighter pulled Captain Hunt above the raging waters and into the arms of the other firefighters.

Peering out of the fire truck's massive windows, the panic-stricken mother watched as the firefighters started to climb down the mountain from the top of the Esker, the life basket between them. At the same moment, the firefighters dragged Captain Hunt from the rain-swollen ravine. The lightning lit Julia Road Park in a massive burst of light as a bolt of lightning struck near second base off to the left of the rescue scene. At that moment, the mother knew her son was not coming out of the pipe alive, as she could see there was no child in the arms of the firefighters. She began to weep. The rain calmed for a moment; the wind came to an eerie quiet as the cold wind from the Atlantic Ocean that whipped over the top of the Esker had stopped, leaving a chilling calm over the rescue scene.

Climbing out of the ravine, Firefighter Tobin bent over, gasping for breath as Captain Hunt was carried quickly to a waiting ambulance.

"What happened in their firefighter?" Looking up the young firefighter saw the town's fire chief standing over him. "I need your report firefighter," the fire chief snapped out as he watched the crew finish their climb down the Esker. Turning back towards firefighter Tobin, the fire chief again said, "Report."

"Captain Hunt found the child about 60 feet into the right storm drain. It appeared the child was dead according to the captain." Gasping to catch his breath, the young firefighter stood up and continued. At this point the captain tried to secure the child's body for extraction, but something grabbed the child and started to drag the boy deeper into the storm drain. Captain Hunt yelled for me to pull as he tried to secure the child by grabbing the child's leg. At this point, I yelled out for the team to also pull us out. Grabbing the captain by his safety harness, I began to pull us towards the entrance of the storm drain. After a moment, the captain went limp and I continued to pull us out. Due to the captain's injuries I did not think I could pursue the child any further at that point."

"It has not been a good day that is for sure," the fire chief yelled out as he continued to look over the young firefighter's shoulder watching the water rise in the ravine. "This rescue attempt is over for today. Tomorrow it turns into a recovery mission for the child's body. Did the other team find the police officer?"

The young firefighter called out as he watched the ambulance doors slam shut. "Yes, they found him dead in the drain like the child. Something had gotten hold of him and whatever it was did not leave a pretty sight of what was left of the officer."

Looking back towards the ambulances, the fire chief could see both of the rigs were starting to move out. The ambulances had started the wailing of sirens in a high- pitched scream as if they needed to get to somewhere in a hurry. The dead were in no hurry, but protocol was protocol.

Shaking his head ever so slightly, the chief turned back towards the shivering young firefighter Tobin. "Go get dried off firefighter. And you did the right thing; there was nothing else you could have done given the circumstances."

The heavy rain continued its steady, maddening downpour. The sound of thunder had started to echo in the distance. The crack of lightning filled the dark sky overhead, bathing the ball field in an eerie black and white macabre picture for such a brief instant.

The scream of the ambulances' sirens could barely be heard now as the ambulances left the park. The young firefighter began to shiver. Was it the cold, or what had just happened? Looking over towards the ravine, the young firefighter watched for a moment as if the child might appear.

But knew the child was gone as the ocean water began to overflow into the ball park hiding any signs of the massive storm drain.

"Chief, can I be of any assistance?"

Turning towards the sound of the voice, firefighter Tobin saw Father Gilday of the local Catholic parish walking towards the fire chief. The old priest in his black outfit and a long scarf around his neck to help ward of the cold, walked hunched over in the madding rain-storm.

"Yes, Father, thank you for coming so quickly," replied the chief, turning the priest towards the fire truck where Mrs. McGrath sat waiting for the news of her son. "I have some bad news for the mother of the child lost in the storm drain. It appears the child has died from drowning and the weather is making recovery of the body impossible at this time."

Turning back to look at the swollen storm drain, the young fire fighter knew the drowning part was to ease the pain of the mother; to tell her something had ripped her child apart would not be in the interest of anyone right now, especially the mother. The sound of the agonizing screams of a parent filled the air as the mother climbed down from the fire truck into the waiting arms of the priest. The rain continued at a steady downpour. Looking towards the sky, Father Gilday held the mother as the pain and her tears fell and mixed with the never-ending rain.

> *O Lord, grant those who have died the joy of Your Presence,*
> *and us who are living the happiness of knowing this.*

Praying softly the priest held the sobbing mother as she collapsed from the pain.

For the next two days, a recovery mission of the storm drains and search of the marsh behind the Esker failed to find any sign of the body of the McGrath boy. A few days later while walking his dog, a local man found the severed foot of a child in a bloodstained white sneaker in the right field of the baseball park. The McGrath family confirmed the sneaker as one of Tommy's.

1975

"**S**TRIIIIIKE ONE!" THE ANNUAL Little League baseball game was underway... the police department's team of kids against the fire department's team of kids. Every Fourth of July, this game was played out at the Julia Road Park playground; this year was going to be a heck of a game. The town of Weymouth was in full party mode, celebrating its three--hundred-forty-fourth birthday today, and along with the country's birthday, it promised to be a wicked lot of fun for all involved.

Many of the parents of the kids playing ball had planned to make it a full day at the park. With the cookouts, organized games for the kids, and fireworks later that evening, the day promised to be fun for all the families at the park. Besides, the round= robin baseball tournament promised to consume most of the day, and for Patty Bertholdi, the mother of the right fielder on the police team, ten-year-old Adam Bertholdi, it promised to be an extra-long day, as the police team was wicked well and would probably go far into the baseball tournament.

Sadly, Adam was not that good and was banished to right field as most of the kids batted right-handed and never hit a ball into right field. But hey, he's on a winning team, his mother thought as the umpire yelled, *STRIIIIIKE TWO!"*

"Umpire! Time!" Walking to the batter's box, Coach Tobin of the fire department's team needed to have a word with Roy Long, his current batter.

Bending down on one knee, the coach came eye to eye with the boy. "Hey, Roy, how are you feeling today?"

"Not bad, Coach," was the reply from the nine-year-old batter.

"Well, do you suppose you could hit the ball for me today? This pitcher is throwing nothing but fast strikes." Standing up, the coach patted Roy on the head and then turned and headed back toward the bench at a brisk trot.

"Will do, Coach!" the young batter yelled out. Turning back toward the pitcher, Roy started to dig his back foot in as the next pitch was going somewhere and the catcher was not part of his plan.

"Play ball!" Pulling his mask down, the umpire got low behind the catcher.

Out on the pitcher's mound, the police department's best pitcher, eleven-year-old Chris Baker, got ready to throw his next pitch. Looking toward the catcher behind the plate for the pitch sign, the young pitcher got what he wanted; the split finger sign meaning a fast ball. Nodding his head slightly, Chris got ready to throw the only pitch he really knew. Looking one more time toward the plate, the young pitcher started his long throwing stretch move toward the plate, tossing the baseball as hard as he could at the end of the stretch. Crouching at the plate in a perfect batter stance, Roy watched the moving fastball travel straight down the pipe just like coach said. Digging his back foot into the dirt around home plate, he swung his Louisville Slugger bat for all of it was worth at the fast moving ball.

Crack! The fastball and the bat hit in perfect contact, sending the ball high and into deep right field over the first baseman's head. The ball continued in a high arc deeper into the right field. Groans and cheers filled the air from the parents, and some of the parents cheered as the ball continued its flight into right field. But other parents groaned, and the mother of right fielder Adam was among them. She knew her son was about to be ridiculed for missing this catch.

The parents began to yell, *"Adam, Adam! Catch the ball!"* Adam was not much of a ball player. He never really liked sports, but his parents had pushed the young boy to try to make him fit the mold his father had in mind. Sadly, for the father of this eight-year-old, it was not to be. Lacking any athletic ability, the young boy fumbled with anything that had to do with sports and hated playing baseball.

As the child's grandfather would say, "Adam is not built to play sports." Watching a dragonfly dance on the high grass as the sun splashed its warmth on the field, the last thing Adam had on his mind was the baseball game being played at that moment.

Hearing the screams of his mother, *"Adam, Adam! Heads up! Heads up! Here comes the ball!"* he looked toward her. He saw her jumping up and down over by the third base line and pointing toward him. The coaches, players, and other parents' voices were screaming out his name, *"Adam, catch the ball!"* The screams of his mother continued, *"Adam! Heads up; catch the ball!"* The stunned child looked up just in time to see the sharply hit-baseball fly over his head and continue its flight path, dropping into the high grass about twenty feet behind him.

"Ground rule double, Ground rule double! The ball is in the high grass!" his mother yelled. She added hopefully, "Thank God Adam wasn't at fault for the double since no play is allowed in the high grass. The rules state no play in the high grass."-Looking toward the umpire, Adam's mother was rewarded with the umpire shouting ground rule double, ordering the advancing runner to stop at second base.

"Hey, Adam! Adam, go get the ball!" ten-year-old Justin Fowler, the center fielder, screamed from his center field position. "Get the ball so we can keep playing!"

"Shut up, Justin. I know how to play baseball," the young right fielder snapped back at Justin.

"Careful, Adam, you punk…your mother won't be here later."

Understanding the threat, Adam nodded to the center fielder, turned and ran into the high grass. Kicking around, he quickly found the ball and looked toward the center fielder, yelling, "Found it!" Adam bent down to pick up the dirty baseball.

Watching her son run to retrieve the ball, his mother gave a sigh of relief. Her son's team could lose every game for all she cared. The only thing that mattered was that Adam wasn't the reason for the loss.

"Hey, Patty, good game so far."

Adam's mother didn't need to turn around as she watched her son bend over in the high sea grass to pick up the baseball, already knowing the voice was that of center fielder Justin's mother, Donna.

"Hey, Donna, how's your day going?" Patty was never really sure if she and Donna where friends or bitter rivals. Both had attended Weymouth High in the 60s, got married to high school sweet-hearts, and got pregnant about a year apart. Sadly, for Patty, motherhood had not been kind to her body, while motherhood seemed not to affect Donna's body at all, and she still had the stunning figure she'd had in her high school years.

"My day is going fine; and yours?" Not waiting for an answer to her question, Donna continued chatting away. "Boy, Adam was lucky on that play."

"What do you mean by that remark?" Patty turned, arms folded across her chest.

Damn, Donna was dressed to kill today. Short hot pants and a tank top that did not hide much. Anyone watching this exchange would give it to Donna on looks alone.

"Well, I'm just saying the reason Adam is in right field is because he really isn't that good at baseball." Again not waiting for a response, she continued her rant. "Heck, I told Justin to stay close to Adam and give him advice on how to play the ball if it came his way. Never thought it would, though. What is going on in right field?" Donna asked, shading her eyes from the sun to get a better view of right field. "Patty, where did Adam go?" she asked as she continued to scan for the young right fielder.

"What are you talking about? He must be out there somewhere." Scanning right field, Patty could not see her eight-year-old son.

"Justin! Go help Adam find the ball!" Donna screamed out, pointing toward right field.

"On it, Mom! Adam, Adam, quit playing around." Starting to jog that direction, Justin called out again, "C'mon, Adam, quit playing around!"

Reaching the point where he had last seen Adam, Justin bent down and picked up the dirty baseball. Standing back up, the older boy looked around a bit before turning toward his mother and yelling, "Adam isn't here, but I found the baseball."

Throwing the ball toward the infield, Justin started a slow trot back to his center field position.

Twenty-six-year-old Ryan Gallagher was the newest (and first) park ranger for Great Esker Park. Tall and lanky, having never quite filled out, Ryan was given the nickname Stick in high school and it stayed with him. Fresh out of an eight-year tour in the army, Ryan was anxious to put army life and Vietnam behind him. Jobs were scarce for a returning veteran at the time. Luckily, a friend of his parents had some pull with the Weymouth

Parks Department and landed Ryan a full time job as one of Great Esker Park's two rangers and tour guides. There was little to do on this holiday weekend in Esker Park, so why not catch a good game of local baseball? Ryan knew most of the kids playing today in some form or another, either through older siblings or their parents. North Weymouth was still a small part of the town of Weymouth, and most folks knew each other personally.

"Hey, *Stick*, how are you? I didn't know you were back from the army."

Ryan turned to see his old high school sweetheart, Debbie Wisdom, holding a baby on her hip. Smiling a bit, he replied, "Hey, Debbie. Yes, I got out about a month ago."

Debbie tiptoed up and kissed Ryan on his cheek. "It's good to see you back safe," she whispered in his ear.

"Glad to be here safe, Debbie," Ryan replied. Then he paused, looking at the baseball diamond. The game had stopped, and something was going on in right field.

"He's not there! I looked twice!" the center fielder yelled out, indicating the area of right field he'd been to a few minutes earlier trying to find Adam. Moving back and forth he continued moving the high grass around with his baseball glove. After a few moments, he yelled out again, "He's not out here!"

"Bring it in, Justin. Everyone, bring it in!" Coach Hammond yelled out, waving at his team to leave the field and head toward the bench.

Justin trotted toward his coach. "Telling ya, Coach, Adam's not out in the field," he said as he stopped briefly in front of Coach Hammond. "I bet he went home because he missed the ball and could have cost us the game," Justin continued as he moved past the coach and disappeared into the crowd of players.

Adam's mother had stopped listening to Donna and was now walking, slowly at first; toward the last place, she had seen her son. "Adam! Adam, stop playing around! Let's get the game going!" Stopping for a moment, Adam's mother looked over toward her son's team bench to make sure he had not somehow sneaked back without her seeing him. Sensing something had happened to her child, Patty quickened her pace toward right field.

Coach Hammond was pretty sure there was no way for his young right fielder to sneak away without being seen. The high grass Adam had disappeared into backed up to the Esker and it was an open, steep climb to reach the top. The child could have not climbed the Esker without being seen. To the left of the grass was open center field and no place to hide. To the right of the grass was also an open field, so the child had to still be in the grass.

"Coach Wilson, keep the team here," Hammond called out to the assistant coach. Looking across the field toward the fire department team, he caught the eye of Coach Tobin, and with a nod toward right field, headed toward the high grass.

Catching the look of concern from the police department's team coach. Coach Tobin of the fire department's team also started toward the right field grass where the child was last seen. Off to the coach's right, he could see the missing right fielder's mother heading that way as well. Her pace had quickened with fear.

"Coach Longo, keep the team here on the bench," Tobin yelled over his shoulder as he started a slow trot to get ahead of the mother in the right field grass. It would not do for her to find the child hiding first, as the young right fielder would probably get a whooping.

Arriving to the grassy area first, Coach Hammond called out, "Adam! Adam, where are you?! Adam! Adam, enough playing around!"

Nearing the area, the young right fielder's mother picked up the chant. "Let's go, Adam! Stop playing around!."

"Any luck finding him?" Coach Tobin called out as he slowed his trot to a standstill next to Coach Hammond.

"Not a sign of him. He was right here picking up the baseball last I saw him." He looked toward the Esker a few feet away. "Well, he couldn't have climbed up the Esker without us seeing him, so he must still be in this grass somewhere," Coach Hammond concluded, more to himself than to the handful of parents who had started to gather around the spot in right field.

"Well, let's spread out and find him so we can get the game going," Coach Tobin called out as he walked away from the crowd toward the Esker, moving the high grass with his hands as he went. He wasn't quite sure why, but Coach Tobin had a bad feeling about this and knew time mattered in finding this child. The couldn't shake the feeling that something was wrong. Pushing the grass aside a bit more, he came to a small ravine that he'd seen years before; the storm drain eight-year-old Tommy McGrath had never came out of years ago was at the end of the ravine that ran under the Esker. At the opening of the storm drain lay a small baseball glove.

On the third base side of the baseball diamond, an older man in his fifties wearing a Boston Red Sox cap began to shake in his lawn chair. Watching the crowd of parents running over to right field could only mean one thing, and over there was the storm drain. "Dear God, not again," the man said to himself. Reaching down, he touched what-remained of his left hand. Then retired Weymouth Firefighter Captain Hunt got up from his lounge chair and started to walk toward the growing crowd out in right field.

"This isn't good," Coach Hammond said, stopping just short of falling into the rocky ravine. Like Firefighter Tobin, Officer Hammond also had harsh memories of this storm drain; Coach Hammond was a rookie police officer that grim summer of 1964 when the little McGrath boy and Sergeant Giannone were brutally attacked and killed in this storm drain. Starting to shake a bit, the coach recalled Sergeant Giannone's hideous screams a few moments after he'd gone into the massive storm drain to rescue the screaming child. Hammond spied the baseball glove near the opening to the massive storm drain. "Do you think he went in there?" Hammond said, turning to Coach Tobin.

"I don't think he went in there on his own, if that's what you are asking," Tobin replied. Half sliding and half walking, he entered the ravine and picked up the baseball glove. Bending down a bit, the coach looked into the dark opening, and the memory of what had happened to the McGrath boy and Captain Hunt rushed back from somewhere deep in his mind; a place where hidden nightmares stay. Was this nightmare going to start again? Hearing a woman scream, Tobin was startled back to the present.

"That's Adam's glove! Did you find him?"

Turning toward the frantic voice, Coach Tobin already knew it was the young boy's mother.

"Is Adam in that drain?!" Continuing down the side of the ravine, she rushed up and grabbed the glove from Tobin. "It *is* Adam's glove!" Bending down and peering into the darkness, she screamed, "Adam, get your ass out here right now!" The echo of Adam's name bounced endlessly through the massive pipe without reply as the mother began weeping. Turning toward

Coach Tobin with panic now gripping her, she pleaded, "I know my son is in there! You're a firefighter. Please help my son!" Turning back toward the drain, she again screamed her son's name. "Adam, Adam!" Again, the only response was her own desperate voice echoing his name off the endless cold concrete walls deep under the Esker.

"I'm sure Adam must have just gone home, Mrs. Bertholdi. He wouldn't have gone into the storm drain, of that I'm pretty sure, Coach Hammond said quietly as he helped the mother of the young right fielder to her feet, knowing full well that the only place the child could have gone without being seen was into the drain. "Why don't you go home and see if he's there. We'll keep looking around here just to make sure."

Looking toward the growing crowd at the edge of the ravine, Coach Hammond called out, "Donna, can you go with Mrs. Bertholdi and wait until we find out something, or come back if Adam is home?"

"Will do, Coach," she called out as she extended her hand to help the other mother climb out of the ravine. "Come on, Patty. Let's head up to your place and see if Adam's there yet." With her arm around Adam's mother, she started a quick pace out of the field toward Elva Road, where the Bertholdi family lived.

"Coach Tobin, Coach Hammond, a word with you two if you don't mind!" a voice called down from the edge of the ravine.

Before he even turned around, Tobin knew the voice of his longtime friend, Fire Chief Commander Butch Hunt. They had become friends over the years since, as a rookie firefighter, Tobin had entered this very storm drain in search of a young boy that summer afternoon in 1964 along with then Captain Hunt. The search and rescue results were two dead. The young McGrath boy, Tommy, and Weymouth Police Officer Nick Giannone both perished that day. The police officer had been badly mauled by something in the drain, and only Captain Hunt saw the McGrath boy before he vanished into the bowels of the storm drains. Something in the drain had snatched the child's body from Captain Hunt's grasp in that drain, dragging the boy deeper into the cold blackness. The child's body was never recovered, and Captain Hunt never talked about the condition of the boy.

"Sure thing, Captain Hunt!" Tobin called out, turning the edge of the ravine.

Climbing up, Tobin and Hammond became aware of a growing number of parents and players from both teams who were starting toward the ravine to see what was going on. Some of the parents had stopped for a moment to talk briefly with Patty Bertholdi, and the crowd around the ravine was starting to grow.

"Good morning, Captain Hunt. Good to see you" reaching out with his hand, Tobin shook Hunt's hands.

"Hey, Paul, good to see you, too," Hunt replied. "Paul, you need to get these people doing something else right now." Looking toward the crowd of parents and players walking toward them, the captain continued, "Have them start searching the Esker and the streets around here. The last thing we need is a panic."

Looking down into the ravine, Captain Hunt shuddered a bit as the painful memories of that afternoon and the consequences that followed flooded back into his conscious. Reaching down, he rubbed what remained of his mangled left hand, a grim reminder of what had happened on the day Tommy McGrath disappeared in the storm drains.

"Right, Captain; will do," Coach Tobin replied as he turned toward the group heading into right field. "Listen up, folks!" he yelled out, raising his hands in the air to halt the oncoming parents and players a few feet short of the ravine. "Folks, listen up! Coach Hammond and I are sure Adam is fine and either went home or is hiding around here or up on the Esker. Isn't that right, Coach Hammond?"

Walking up to stand beside Tobin, Hammond nodded and added, "What we need right now is to make sure we cover all the bases here." A few of the players smiled and laughed a bit at the baseball reference to the search that was about to begin. "We need to search the Esker and a few streets around the ballpark. So let's break up into three groups and do just that. Coach Longo, Coach Wilson, can you both come over here for a moment?" He called out, waving the coaches through the crowd of parents and players.

Waiting for the coaches to make their way through the crowd, Hammond turned to Tobin and Hunt and spoke quietly so only the two of them could hear what he had to say. "So, who will search the storm drain?"

As Hammond looked down into the ravine at the storm drain entrance, he could hear the screams of Nick Giannone in his mind like it was today. He shuddered.

Watching Hammond staring at the drain, Hunt knew there was no way the police officer could head in there to do the necessary search for the young ball player. "Paul, you up to another trip?"

"Let's hope it's not necessary," Tobin replied as he turned Longo and Wilson, who were just arriving "OK, Coach Longo, will take a few of your parents and players and head up on the Esker and down to the Hingham Bridge and back."

"Will do. I need about five folks with me," Longo called out, waving at the group of parents and players. Heading off toward a trail that snaked up the Esker, he was followed by five or six parents and their kids.

Turning to Wilson, Tobin shouted above the increasing noise of the crowd, "Coach, I need you to take a group up the Esker to the town dump and check out Reversing Falls, then head back here, please."

Nodding his understanding, Coach Wilson then headed off toward the trails that led up to the top of the Esker. A group of parents and their children turned and followed.

Off to the right, entering the ballpark, Coach Tobin could see a Weymouth police cruiser slowly making its way toward the crowd.

"I guess Adam wasn't at home, and his mother called the police," Hammond said, watching the black and white come to a stop next to the ravine.

"Got a call reporting a lost child?" Patrol Officer Peter Collins queried, stepping out of the police unit.

Walking toward the group of coaches, he took out a small notebook and read the description from the lost child report. "White male child, eight years old, name Adam Bertholdi. Dressed in a blue baseball uniform with the letters WPD on the shirt. This child was last seen playing baseball at the Julia Road Park baseball diamond. I take it the child hasn't been found yet?"

Recognizing Senior Police Officer Sergeant Hammond, Collins called out to him, "You don't think he went into that storm drain, do you?"

"Not sure. We have two search parties up on the Esker looking right now," Coach Hammond replied.

"Officer, do you have a flashlight in your cruiser?"

Officer Collins knew at once it was retired Captain Hunt asking, he turned and answered, "Right away, Captain Hunt. I have a nice search and rescue light in the trunk." Collins quickly returned with the powerful flashlight. "Here you go, Captain."

"I got it, Captain," Tobin said, taking the powerful flashlight from the police officer and starting back down the ravine, shaking his head ever so slightly. This is something he'd never wanted to do again, but a child's life might be at stake.

"What are the chances that whatever was in the storm drain all those years ago would still be there?" Tobin said, clicking the powerful flashlight on and off.

"Paul, just go to the intersection and flash the light down the three tunnels," Hunt called out, coming up to stand next to his young friend at the opening "The chances of that thing still being around after all these years is slim to none I should think," he spoke in a hopeful tone as he bent down peering into the darkness.

"Yes, just what I was planning to do the child did go in the drain for some reason, I don't think he would go very far to hide," Tobin replied, praying the child had not gone in there.

"Well, at least there is little chance of drowning today," Hammond added, as he, too, bent down to peer into the drain.

Turning on the powerful flashlight, Tobin got on his hands and knees, just like all those years ago, and entered the storm drain.

BACK INTO THE STORM DRAINS

THE CONCRETE WALLS OF the storm drain were cold and rough to the touch, even though the dog days of summer were upon this coastal town. The drains never seemed to retain any heat, being so far underground. All these years later, the drain hadn't changed one bit.

"Well, at least it's not raining this time," Tobin called out over his shoulder to Hunt, who was kneeling at the entrance, scanning the darkness intently for signs of the child or demon that had haunted the tunnels so many years ago.

Laughing a bit, the captain replied, "Yes, but wearing those shorts will get your knees pretty scraped up. Get in, find the child, and get out. Keep focused on the mission. I'll keep you in sight at all times. Do you get that, firefighter?" Hunt yelled to make the point that Coach Tobin was now Weymouth Firefighter Tobin, and the mission of searching this storm drain came with a grave risk of death.

Knowing full well what Captain Hunt meant, Tobin yelled over his shoulder, "Understood, sir; focus on the mission." The sound of slowly dripping water pierced the silence of the darkness in front of him.

"Heck, the kid is probably at home hiding in his bedroom closet," Hunt said, more to himself as a vain hope. He glanced Looking up toward the top of the ravine for some sign the young ball player had been found, but there was none.

Tobin slowly moved deeper into the darkness. Once again, like so many years before, the flashlight was barely making a dent in the cool, pitch black darkness of the storm drain. The air in the storm drain was thick with the salty smell of the costal marshes, mud flats, and spike grasses that ran the length of the Esker on the seaward side of the 12,000-year-old glacier.

Moving slowly, the Atlantic breeze came down the Weymouth Back River, and into the salt marsh mudflats, pushing the smells and sounds of the marsh into the drains that ran under the Esker. The tide was low, and the screams of sea-gulls' signaling that the many fish left behind when the tide receded were now dinner could be heard echoing through the.

Entering the intersection of the three drains, the firefighter paused for a moment to get his bearings. Flashbacks of the past and even the noise of slowly dripping water were forcing the firefighter to slow his breathing again to control the panic threatening to overcome him.

The curved concrete walls seemed to be closing in as the screams of the past seemed to fill this place even now. "Focus, Tobin," he said softly to himself, trying to stay quiet so the past horrors might not know he had returned to this terrible place of death under the Esker.

Flashing the powerful beam of light into the tunnel to his left, all the firefighter could see for twenty or so yards was empty blackness. A small stream of water quietly flowed back toward the salt marsh unlike the past, when the water was like a rushing freight train. The beam of light bounced off the walls of concrete and disappeared into the endless darkness. The missing child did not appear to be in that drain.

"Nothing in the left tunnel!" he called over his left shoulder to the small crowd at the opening. Swinging the light around, Tobin began to search the right storm drain the one where Captain Hunt had fought a life and death struggle to save a child years ago.

There seemed to be slight movement in the salty blackness about thirty feet ahead-and Tobin cautiously crawled forward as the beam of light cast an eerie glow. The taste of dry salt in the air was nauseating, and with his heart pounding in fear, the firefighter fought hard to control his labored breathing and focus on the mission of finding the lost child.

He could feel the walls of the tunnel closing in on him but the movement seemed to be staying just out of reach of the light. After ten more feet of crawling, the firefighter knew the child would never be found alive.

Reaching forward, the firefighter grabbed hold of a child's baseball cap. The initials WPD were on the brim of the cap and the name Adam

Bertholdi was written in bold black lettering on the inside Tobin began to slowly, cautiously back out of the storm drains. The essence of evil and death that had been here so many years ago was still lurking in the darkness of the drains.

Coming out!" he called over his shoulder. Clutching the baseball cap, Tobin quickens his backward pace as panic and fear once again closed around him. Keeping the powerful beam of light pointed back down the drain, he was certain something was moving toward him but staying just out of reach of illumination.

"What's going on?" Park Ranger Ryan Gallagher asked the group of people who were now gathering around the storm drain.

"It seems we have got another missing child in the storm drain" an older man spoke out, continuing to look down.

"Bob, the last thing we need right now is someone spreading rumors," Captain Hunt called up from the mouth of the drain down in the shallow ravine.

"Rumors? Really? It seems like the McGrath boy all over again if you ask me," Bob Crosby called back down.

"The McGrath boy?" The young park ranger asked.

"Back in 64, I think it was, Tommy McGrath, eight years old at the time, took a dare and went into the storm drains to see if he could go from the other side of the Esker to this side. He never made it through."

"What happened?" Ryan asked, moving closer to the older man, who continued the story.

"The official account is drowning, but the body of the child was never recovered."

"A police officer, Giannone I think was his name, died in the rescue attempt. Something in the drain mauled him pretty badly. He had a closed casket funeral and the official cause of death was never released to the public."

The old man turned to Gallagher. "During the rescue attempt, Captain Hunt lost most of his left hand to whatever was in the drain." Crosby was suddenly stopped short by a woman's scream.

"That's Adam's baseball cap! That's Adam's cap!" Patty Bertholdi had seen Tobin emerges from the storm drain with the tattered cap and hand it to Hunt.

"Any sign of the child in there?" Hunt asked, taking the baseball cap for a closer inspection.

"Not sure. I went in as planned and searched the left drain first. But I saw some sort of movement, or more like I sensed movement, about twenty feet into the right drain," Tobin spoke, reaching down to wipe the dirt from his bloodied knees. Looking up, he saw Adam's panicky mother sliding down the side of the ravine.

"Can I see that cap please?" she demanded. Grabbing the cap from Captain Hunt, she flipped it over. "I always write Adam's name on the inside of his caps." Turning the cap over, she made the grim discovery.

"This *is* Adam's cap! See, here is his name." She held the cap out to Captain Hunt.

"Yes, that says Adam Bertholdi," Hunt said as he took the cap back from Patty. Examining the cap more closely, Captain Hunt could not help but notice the top of the cap was crushed and split open, and what appeared to be blood and hair fragments surrounded the edges of the tear.

"Are you sure Adam is not at home, Mrs. Bertholdi?" Hunt asked the frantic mother, already knowing the answer.

"Yes, I'm sure. I searched the house from top to bottom, and he's not there. I called Adam's father and he's on his way," the frantic mother replied. Then she yelled out:, "He must be in that drain." Lunging forward, she screamed out her child's name. "Adam, Adam! Get out here now!"

"Donna come down here, please, and take Mrs. Bertholdi back to her house to wait for her husband," Tobin called out to the woman at the edge of the ravine.

"Sure thing, Paul; no problem." She spoke softly to Patty while turning her away from the silence and darkness of the storm drain.

"It's OK, Patty; they'll find Adam. Let's go home and look around a bit for Adam in case he came home while we wait for your husband."

"The hat looks pretty torn up, Captain. Like some sort of blunt object hit the head," Tobin spoke out as he took the cap and turned it over a few times. Handing it back to the captain, he added, "Almost like something struck him in the head and then pulled back, yanking hair and skin off his head."

"Whatever was in that drain last time appears to still be there." Tobin spoke quietly to Hunt, turning back toward the drain as if whatever was in there might soon emerge.

"That is more than just hair and skin That's also bone fragments," Hunt said as he wrapped a white handkerchief around the cap. He motioned for Officer Collins to come closer.

"Officer, this ball cap is now evidence; please make sure it is treated as such." Handing the cap to the police officer, Hunt turned toward the edge of the ravine.

"Will do, Cap," Collins replied. "I'll get it in an evidence bag right way."

Looking up at the growing crowd, Captain Hunt could see that both of the search parties from the Esker had returned. Neither appeared to have had any luck.

"Coach Longo, Coach Wilson, did you find any sign of him?" He called out to the two men and their search teams as they approached the side of the ravine.

"We went down to the Hingham Bridge, but no sign of him," Coach Longo called out. We took the Back River all the way back to Reversing Falls from here, and no sign there, either."

"Same here," Coach Wilson reported. "All the way to the dump and back along the beaches past Wale Island and up the marsh flats to here. No sign of the child."

Captain Hunt was now painfully aware that the crowds around the storm drain and at the edge of the ravine had gone silent. The murmuring and speculation about where the child may be had stopped. Everyone knew where the child had to be, and the stunned crowd looked to him for what to do next.

"Collins, call in and report we have a child lost and maybe trapped under the Esker," Captain Hunt called out to the police officer.

MISSING CHILD

THE SOUND OF SCREAMING sirens cracked the silence the air around the ballpark. Officer Collins had begun moving the crowd back from the shallow ravine as the first fire rescue unit entered the park from the Elva Road entrance. A second unit and another patrol car enter through the main entrance on Julia Road. Confusion reigned at first.

"Excuse me, do you have a moment?" Ryan Gallagher called down into the ravine to Hunt and Tobin, who where still standing at the entrance to the storm drain.

"Sure. What can we do for you?" Tobin called and waved the park ranger to come down.

"Well, I'm the park ranger for the Esker. My name is Ryan Gallagher." Reaching out, the park ranger shook the firefighter's hand.

"Glad to meet you, Ryan. I'm Paul Tobin, and this old man is Butch Hunt, retired firefighter super star."

"Glad to meet you, Ryan," Captain Hunt said, stepping forward to shake the park ranger's hand. "What can we do to help you, Ryan?" Hunt asked as he turned toward the ravine, watching as Officer Collins continued to move the crowd back from the edge.

"Paul, I need to get up top and make sure the rescue units are ready when they get here. From the sound of the sirens, I would say that's within the next minute." Turning toward the ravine, Hunt started a quick walk up the side and Collins held out his hand to help pull him up.

"Got two rescue units coming, Cap, and two patrol units to help with the crowd," he shouted over the deafening wail of sirens from emergency fire units and police cars flooding into Julia Road Park.

Back down in the ravine, Ryan turned to Tobin. "I'd like to offer any help I can." Looking toward the storm drain opening, the park ranger continued. "It seems you folks think he's in that drain somewhere" Bending over, he peered deep into the cool salty thick darkness.

"Not really sure, but it seems the only place left to look," Tobin said coming over to the drain. He squatted down and continued, "The last time I went into this drain to look for a child, years ago, things did not turn out so well."

"So I heard, from a local resident a few minutes ago." Ryan Gallagher spoke as he continued to gaze into the blackness of the drain, where there seemed to be movement, if ever so slight. Based more on instinct from a tour of duty in combat than hard facts, Gallagher was sure something was watching them from deep within the tunnels of the drain "Paul, you and the park ranger get up here please," Captain Hunt called down, motioning for the men to come up to the small group of police and locals who had gathered around the ravine's edge.

"Well, we'd better get a move on. The captain does not like to ask twice," Tobin said, slapping the park ranger on the shoulder. Turning toward the group of men, the two climbed up.

Tobin noticed units one and two of the Weymouth Fire Department had been dispatched to the scene and were slowly making their way over, being very careful of the swarming crowd in the field that seemed to getting larger by the moment.

Captain Hunt was already giving out orders as the firefighter and park ranger approached the group of men and women. Everybody were listening intently.

Walking up to the two search teams that had just returned from the Esker, Tobin smiled a bit and said to Gallagher, "Even in retirement, Captain Hunt is in charge of any emergency wherever he is.

I'm pretty sure he'll be in charge even in death." Smiling, he turned his attention to the commands Hunt was now issuing to the crowd.

"All right; once again, the same search teams are to go back up on the Esker," Hunt called out to the coaches who had led the last search. Coach Longo, extend your search to Stodder's Neck and back under the Hingham Bridge."

"Will do, Captain. Stodder's Neck and back under the Hingham Bridge,"Longo called out as he turned and waved his search team to follow him back up the Esker.

"Coach Hammond, take your search team down to the other side of the town dump and then along Back River, and give Whale Island a good look over," Hunt called out to the other team's coach.

"On it, Captain Hunt!" Hammond called out. Motioning for his search team to follow, the coach turned toward the Esker.

"And this time, slow it down a bit and start looking for clues the child had been up there. Then report back here." Motioning toward the Esker with a wave, Captain Hunt yelled out, "Let's go get a move on; and be safe!"

The gigantic fire units pulled to a halt a short distance from the group. The massive air brakes wailed out a hissing sound as the fire rigs stopped. The diesel engines slowed to idle as the firefighters climbed down and grabbed their equipment off the trucks for the next mission. The group of ten firefighters headed toward the ravine and Captain Hunt, rescue equipment in hand, ready for the mission of search and rescue under the Esker. They stopped short of the ravine, looking to Captain Hunt for their orders. The retired firefighter knew that a child's life was in the balance so time was precious now.

"All right, unit two, take your men to the other side of the Esker," he said, pointing toward the top of the Esker. "Go to the storm drain entrance, light it up, and wait for further orders.

Unit one will set up here in this ravine down by the storm drain entrance." Hunt paused for a moment as he noticed more and more people were flowing into the ballpark.

"Officer Collins, get the police units to move this crowd out of the park at once," he called out, motioning toward the crowd moving toward the ravine.

"On it, Captain Hunt, Collins replied. All right, officers, let's move this crowd out of the park and give the fire department room to work," he said to the police officers who joined him.

"All searches will start here and end up on the other side of the Esker, with unit two doing the extractions as needed," Hunt yelled down to the rescue unit now setting up operations in the ravine by the entrance to the storm drain.

Turning toward Tobin, Captain Hunt said, "Paul, you up for another search of the drain?" He already knew the answer to his question would be yes.

"Can do, Captain Hunt, on it. Just let me get my gear on," Tobin answered as the quickened his pace and headed toward fire engine one to retrieve his rescue gear.

Pausing for a moment, then added, "Paul, pick out one of your team to back you up in the storm drain."

"Excuse me, Captain Hunt, I would like to back up the firefighter on this rescue mission," Gallagher yelled over the crowd waving at Hunt. Moving through the crowd of firefighters, he stepped forward to face the captain.

"Sure you want to do this, son?" Hunt turned toward the park ranger. "Last time we tried a rescue in storm drains, it didn't go so well for all involved." Looking down into the ravine, Hunt could remember like it was yesterday.

"Sorry I couldn't save you, Tommy," the retired fire chief whispered to the wind. Wiping away a single tears from his face, he turned away from the ravine to help shut out the horror and pain of so many years ago.

Moving toward the park ranger, Captain Hunt put his arm around Ryan's shoulder walked him farther away from the ravine. Continuing in a near whisper so only the park ranger could hear, Hunt continued. "You saw the child's ball cap, right?" The captain said it more as a statement than a question, looking Gallagher right in the eyes.

"Yes I did. You think the child hid in the drain and then was attacked in the there?"

"No, whatever happened to him, it was over in right field and he was carried into the storm drain." Turning to watch fire rescue team two reach the top of the Esker, Captain Hunt continued.

"There were no signs of force or anything being dragged from what I could see in the field where the child was last seen."

Hunt turned back to Gallagher and continued. "But there were a lot of folks running around in the outfield after the child came up missing."

Hunt called out to Tobin, "Paul, the park ranger will be your backup in this search and rescue."

"Hey, Ryan, you sure you want to do this?" Tobin asked, walking over to the park ranger. "Last time, things got real hairy in the drains, and after seeing the boy's ball cap, I'd say it's a safe bet that thing is still in there." Nodding toward the storm drain, the firefighter began the walk down into the ravine. Time was now of the essence, and waiting meant the fear would surface once again, the fear of whatever was in the drain and in all likelihood had claimed its third victim, he thought to himself.

"Hey, Ranger, don't forget a flashlight," Hunt called out, walking toward Ryan. He put the flashlight in Ryan's outstretched hand.

"You're kidding, right? A fun crawl under the Esker." Laughing a bit, the park ranger followed Tobin into the ravine.

"OK, I got the lead into the first tunnel and you take the lead into the second," Tobin said as he bent down, turned on the light, and started to crawl quickly into the darkness.

"Right behind you," Gallagher said, turning on his own flashlight and bending down to follow the firefighter into the massive drain.

Having climbed down the ravine to the storm drain entrance, Captain Hunt bent down on one knee to observe the progress of the search team. He watched the fading beams of light move slowly as the two men made their way deep into the interlaced drains under the Esker. After a moment, the bouncing light disappeared as the two men made the turn into the right storm drain, the same one where he had found the butchered body of the McGrath boy so many years ago.

Time was not on the side of the child if he was under the Esker. Looking over the storm drain to the top of the ravine just above the entrance, Captain Hunt saw a familiar figure, his long colorful scarf draped over his shoulders even on this warm summer day. He stood quietly, performing his solitary duty among all the madness around him.

Father Gilday of the local Catholic parish once again found himself, like so many years ago, standing in this park over this storm drain praying quietly for the soul of a child he already knew was dead.

Lord our God,
you give and you take away.
You blessed us through the gift of this child, Adam,
who is now taken from us
and whose loss we mourn.
Help us, through our tears and pain,
to glimpse your hand at work
to bring blessing out of grief.
To you be glory for-ever.
Amen.

CHILDREN LAUGHING

MOVING QUICKLY INTO THE three-way intersection of storm drains, Tobin paused for a moment. The sound of seagulls from the salt marshes on the other side of the Esker filled the drains with their eerie screams. The taste of dry salt stung his nostrils and made his eyes water. A small steady stream of salt water flowed slowly down the storm drain toward the Back River. An eerie calm filled the tunnel ahead, and the firefighter's powerful beam of light barely illuminated the darkness.

Crawling into the three-way intersection, Gallagher paused for a moment to let his eyes adjust to the salty blackness of the storm drain. The walls were cold and rough to the touch, and he could feel the cold salt water of the Atlantic Ocean seeping slowly into the legs of his pants. The ranger began to follow the bouncing light of the firefighter's flashlight into the right storm drain.

Then Gallagher thought he heard something from the left storm drain and paused for a moment. "Paul, hold up. I think I hear something coming from the other drain."

Slowing his pace, Tobin turned his head toward Gallagher. "What is it?" he asked quietly, as if yelling would alert whatever was in the drains to their presence and location in the endless maze of the drains.

"Not sure, kinda sounds like children laughing and playing," the park ranger said, turning the powerful beam of his flashlight toward the sounds echoing in the other drain to his left.

"Must be from the kids on the ball field," Tobin called out, resuming his slow crawl further into the darkness of the tunnel.

"Yeah; must be kids playing in the field," Gallagher called out in reply, his voice echoing through the drains. Flashing the beam one more time into the left storm drain, the park ranger was about to follow Tobin into the right drain when there appeared to be some sort of movement in blackness of the left tunnel.

Moving slightly forward, Ryan saw something small rolling slowly toward him from the dark drain. The slowly rolling object came to rest a few feet into the beam of his flashlight. It was a baseball, all worn and tattered and soaked with sea water. The word Rawlings could still be made out on the side of the ball.

"Ranger, are you OK?" Tobin asked as he grabbed Ryan's shoulder.

Turning around, Gallagher held his hand up to shield his eyes from the other man's bright light. "Yeah, I'm fine. I heard a noise, and a baseball came rolling down the drain."

Looking past the ranger, Tobin shone his light past the ranger and down the left storm drain. "What baseball? I don't see one," he whispered to Ryan.

Turning around, the park ranger started to point where he had seen the baseball come to a rolling stop. "It's right there..." His voice trailed off as he noticed the ball was now gone. "Well, I *did* see a baseball, with the words Rawlings written on it." Moving a bit forward the park ranger reached out as if the ball might still be there but was somehow hidden in the darkness of the sea water. "Not here now, I guess; but I did see it come rolling down this drain." The ranger started to slowly crawl forward into the blackness of the left storm drain.

"Ryan, hold up a second," Tobin called out.

Stopping for a moment the park ranger turned his head back toward the other man. "Yeah, what you got?" He asked.

The firefighter nodded to where the beam of his flashlight shone on the smooth concrete walls. "What do you make of that?" he said, moving forward to examine something on the wall. As he moved closer, he knew immediately what it was.

"What did you find, Paul?" Ryan asked, moving closer. Then he also saw and recognized what was on the wall.

"It sure looks like a bloody hand print to me," Tobin uttered, moving the light a little closer. He could see the blood trickling down the wall.

"Yeah, and it seems to be fresh blood and the size of a child's hand," Ryan added.–"Did you hear that?" he asked as the sounds of children laughing again seemed to quietly fill the darkness of the storm drain.

"Yeah. That's not outside in the park; that's here in the storm drain," the firefighter whispered in reply. Flashing his powerful light around, Tobin caught a bit of movement coming from the right storm drain. As before, the quiet giggling of children could be heard echoing through the tunnels. "Adam, is that you?" he called out, already knowing the sounds would not be that of the lost child.

"Ryan, you keep searching this drain for another hundred yards, then head back outside," Tobin said, then he began the crawl back to the right storm drain to continue searching it for signs of the child.

"Will do, Paul, one hundred yards and back outside." The park ranger moved forward into the darkness, pushing the powerful flashlight ahead of himself.

Water dripping a warm breeze made it's way off the Back River filling the drain with the smell of the salt marshes. *Crack!* Something hit the park ranger on the forehead.–Fighting to stay conscious, Gallagher saw the baseball rolling toward him from the darkness. When a small hand reached out of the darkness to grab the ball, Ryan reached forward and snatched it, pulling the baseball underneath himself as he began to lose consciousness.

Moving deeper into the right storm drain, Firefighter Tobin was sure something was moving just out of reach of the powerful beam of his flashlight. He was certain he could hear faint sounds up ahead in the darkness, almost like children whispering and giggling as if playing a game of hide and seek with the firefighter.

"Adam Bertholdi, are you there?" He called out, picking up his pace. Something just ahead of him scuffled as it also quickened its pace to avoid the flashlight's beam.

The taste of blood filled the park ranger's mouth, and cold salt water stung the cuts on his face. Pushing himself up out of the water Ryan fought to regain consciousness. The sounds of children's laughter again echoed through the massive storm drain.

Muttering to himself, he reached forward to grab the flashlight that lay on its side in the small stream of ocean water that flowed slowly through the drain. "What the heck hit me?" He muttered to himself. Reaching underneath his body, the ranger pulled out the baseball and held it up into the beam of the flashlight. It was fairly new but was badly dented and wet from being in the storm drain. Turning the ball around, he saw the word Rawlings printed on it.

Crash! Something again knocked the flashlight out of his grasp. As the flashlight crashed against the concrete walls, the light went out and the park ranger found himself in total darkness. A low growling sound quietly started to fill the blackness of the storm drain.

"Dead end," the firefighter said in frustration. The storm drain had come to an end. Dirt, gravel, and a boulder blocked the path of going any deeper into the drain. He flashed the light slowly around the debris to where he was sure he had seen movement just a few moments ago. In the bright glare, Tobin noticed something partially buried in the dirt behind the boulder.

Reaching around, he pulled a small doll in a light blue dress out of the dirt. Holding it up to the beam of light and turning it around slowly, he noticed was very old and showed the wear and tear of being in the storm drain. The firefighter thought it odd, though, that the doll was dry and showed no sign of ever being in the water.

At that moment, a terrible scream echoed through the storm drains.

"Ryan!" Tobin yelled out, dropping the doll as he turned around and started to quickly crawl toward the screams of the park ranger. As the light bounced off the walls fading back down the drain, the boulder he had just left moved ever so slightly and a small hand reached out and grabbed the doll, pulling it quickly behind the boulder.

Something had grabbed the park ranger by the hair in the darkness and was dragging him on his back deeper into the bowels of the drain. Struggling not to panic, Ryan knew he must act quickly, as he was again almost blacking out. Whatever had him by his hair banging his head on the concrete wall as it attempted to drag him deeper into the blackness of the drain.

Reaching for anything to slow the assault, he grabbed the broken flashlight and swung it over his head to hit whatever had him by the hair. A sharp cry of pain echoed in the darkness, and the ranger felt whatever had him by the hair let go for a second. Rolling quickly to his belly, he reared up and swung the flashlight again into the blackness. Again a hit and another hideous scream of pain filled the air.

"Ryan, Ryan, are you OK?" Flashing the powerful beam ahead of him, Tobin entered the left storm drain crawling for all he was worth toward the screaming park ranger. His breath echoed off the concrete wall as the firefighter labored to get enough air into his lungs through the overwhelming thick salty mist and pungent smell of the marsh.

Caught in the approaching glare of the firefighter's flashlight beam, the park ranger was swinging his flashlight at something in front of him. Whatever it was screamed out in pain once again as Ryan repeatedly swung the heavy flashlight madly at the thing.

The thing screaming out again and started to back down into the darkness of the storm drain. But the park ranger was not about to stop the fight. Moving forward, blood streaming down his face, Ryan swung the flashlight again. Again, the hideous scream echoed when the heavy flashlight found its mark once again.

Outside the drain, Captain Hunt listened to the terrorized screams. "Jeff, quick! Get me a light!" he yelled out as another scream rang out of the darkness from the storm drain toward them.

"I'm here, Ryan." Scrambling up behind the park ranger, the firefighter started to flash his light over the park ranger's shoulders to get a better look at whatever it was the ranger was battling. It was a fight the ranger was not winning.

Whatever was attacking Gallagher stopped for a brief moment as the glare of the powerful light filled the tunnel and washed away the blackness that was its cover. It seemed to be man crouched in the drain and covered in some sort of seaweed cloak.

"Ryan, back up slowly!" Tobin called out as he began retreating toward the drain entrance, keeping the creature blinded by the powerful glare of the light.

A low growl filled the tunnel as the creature lifted its head Tobin stopped his movement as the bright yellow eyes of the creature came into focus. Seaweed obscured most of the creature's form, but it was wicked obvious to the firefighter that the thing was pissed. A hideous screech rang out as the creature leaped forward toward the park ranger.

Ryan, watch out!" Tobin yelled out as the creature rushed toward Ryan. But the park ranger was ready this time. Swinging the broken flashlight at the charging creature, his aim was perfect, and the broken glass of the lens cut deep into the creature. The creature backed off for a brief moment as it screamed in pain. Then yowled in rage and lunged once again at Ryan.

Rushing forward on his hands and knees, Tobin jammed his flashlight past the park ranger's shoulder and into the seaweed covered face of the creature. Again, the creature backed off and a horrible scream echoed through the bowels of the drain. But the creature quickly attacked again, lunging at Gallagher and slashing the park ranger's right arm with something just as he'd raised the flashlight to strike at the creature again.

Jamming his own flashlight once again over Gallagher, Tobin felt more than saw the light hit home and cause the creature to again scream out in pain. Pulling back, Tobin once again jammed the light forward with the same results. The creature screamed more loudly and violently this time.

Pulling the light back again, the firefighter sensed the creature was backing off from its attack, and he jammed the light forward again. But this time, the creature had disappeared into the darkness of the storm drains.

"Paul! Paul!" The sound of Captain Hunt's frantic voice was coming closer. The beam of his light showed his frantic pace as it bounced off the smooth concrete walls. He crawled up behind the firefighter and park ranger.

"Something just attacked us! The ranger has been injured, but I'm not sure how bad yet," Tobin called out Hunt.

"I'm fine," Ryan called back. "But I do have something stuck in my right arm, and it's bleeding pretty badly." Lifting his arm into the light to examine it, he added, "I have some sort of seashell embedded deep in my forearm. It feels like it's stuck in the bone."

"OK, let's get you out of here to get medical attention for that arm," Hunt called out as he started to retreat out of the drain. At the intersection of drains, Hunt paused for a moment to stare into the blackness to the right. In all that had happened the last few minutes, he had forgotten all the pain of his last trip here years ago in search of another lost child. And like then, the captain was sure something was watching him from the right storm drain, just beyond the beam of light.

"You OK, Cap?" Backing into intersection, of the three storm drains Tobin paused for a moment to let the captain gather his thoughts and deal with his lingering fears.

"Paul, did you search this side already?" Hunt asked, moving a bit closer to the right and shining the light deeper into the endless pit of blackness.

"Yes, sir. It's blocked off by rocks and dirt about 100 yards in. Looks like the storm drain cracked and the Esker collapsed in," the firefighter replied, motioning for Ryan to climb into the exit storm drain as there was now enough room in the connector for the three men to move around.

Moving past the firefighter, the park ranger kept his right arm raised and slowly crawled out. "You two coming?" He called out, stopping for a moment. His blood dripped down to stain the concrete.

"Yeah, right behind. Let's get that arm attended to," Captain Hunt replied, taking one last look into the right storm drain before turning to follow the park ranger out into the daylight of Julia Road Park.

Tobin continued to look into the right storm drain, wondering if he should check one more time and maybe retrieve the doll he'd found there. Sensing something moving quickly toward him from the left storm drain, he swung his light around and caught a brief glimpse of something covered in seaweed moving quickly away from the glare of the light.

"Paul, get your ass out here now!" Captain Hunt screamed into the storm drain. As he turned toward the entrance, Tobin could again hear the laughter of young children echoing around him.

"On my way now!" he called out, then quickly exited the drain into the bright daylight that washed the park.

WHAT'S GOING ON UP ON THE ESKER?

"LET ME HELP YOU up, Paul," Hunt said as the firefighter came out of the storm drain.

Reaching to take the hand offered by the captain for support, the firefighter struggled to stand after the long, grueling crawl under the Esker.

"Well, Captain, it would seem whatever was there fifteen years ago is still in there," Tobin said, leaning down to examine the many cuts on his bare legs.

"That or something like whatever that thing was," Hunt replied, looking around the top of the ravine for someone. "Here they come now," he said, more to himself than the firefighter. "But whatever it is, we need to find and kill it today," Hunt added with resolve as he reached out to shake Police Deputy Chief Karl Wisdom's hand. The police chief had slid into the ravine, followed by four heavily armed police officers each carrying a shot-gun and wearing a pistol on their hips. Their black jump-suits had the words Weymouth Police Special Units Division on the breast pocket.

"Thanks for the help, Karl. Tobin will fill you in on the storm drain layouts as well as give some insight into what we think is in there. Good luck, officers," Captain Hunt said as he headed toward the side of the ravine to climb out.

"Hey, Cap, where are you going?" Tobin asked as Hunt reached the top of the ravine.

Stopping for a moment, the captain turned back. "You've been in the storm drains more than any of us, and you've seen this thing more than any of us…just give that information to the officers so they can go in and kill it. I need to go check on the park ranger. It's my fault he got hurt; I never should have let him go in there in the first place." Then turning his back on the small group of men, Hunt disappeared over the edge of the ravine.

"OK, officers. Let's see if I can make any sense of this and give you a bit of what I know from my few times in there," Tobin said. Taking a clip board from one of the officers, he drew a rough sketch of the drains under the Esker.

"Ryan, how are you feeling?" Hunt asked, approaching the park ranger, who was sitting in an ambulance. Beside the ranger, a paramedic was gently examining the white crusty object protruding from Ryan's right forearm.

"Good. With the exception of a beat up face and this seashell in my arm, not a bad day at all," Ryan replied, wincing a bit at the pain as the paramedic prodded the object lodged in his arm.

"A seashell?" Hunt asked, climbing into the ambulance to get a better look at it. "Can I see that?" Taking hold of Gallagher's right arm, he slowly moved it around to get a better look at the object. "Yes, more accurately, it's the shell of a quahog, sometimes called a hard-shelled clam. I thought you injured your arm on the wall," the captain said, more to himself than anyone in the back of the ambulance.

"No; whatever attacked me in the drain used the shell as a weapon," Gallagher replied.

"Never heard of an animal using a weapon in an attack," the ambulance attendant chipped in as he started to bandage the wound.

How many times over the years had Captain Hunt and his family dug for these clams in the Back River clam beds at low tide. Several times a year, they had clambakes back home. *Never thought the shells could be used as a weapon,* Captain Hunt thought, letting go of the ranger's arm. The attendant was right; an animal would never use a clamshell as a weapon. "Thanks for the help, Ranger," Hunt called out as he jumped out of the ambulance.

Watching the fire chief quickly walk away, the park ranger's gaze turned toward the Esker. "What the heck is going on up on the Esker?" he uttered.

"Ryan, what happened to you?" a young female voice called from just outside the ambulance door.

Turning around, Ryan saw his assistant park ranger, Kimberly Sarfield. She was about eighteen years old and had the longest ponytail of bright red hair Ryan had ever seen. Fresh out of her senior year at Weymouth North High, this kid loved the Esker and her job.

"Oh, hey, Kimberly. Nothing; just a small cut on my arm." He showed her the clamshell embedded in his forearm.

"Looks more like a quahog clamshell embedded in your arm than a small cut," she commented, laughing a bit. Looking around at the activity in the ball field, she continued, "I hear we have a missing child up on the Esker."

"Not really sure if the child is lost, missing, or just plain hiding from everyone," Ryan answered as the ambulance driver tried to get him to lie down on the stretcher for the ride to the emergency room. "Kim, keep watch for the boy when you do the trash rounds today," Ryan called out as the doors of the ambulance shut.

"Ugh, trash runs," the young park ranger muttered to herself. The three hour trash run consisted of going around the Esker and emptying about fifty trash cans placed at intervals along the six-mile Esker. Since it was summer vacation, most would be loaded with empty beer bottles and cans as local kids used the Esker at night for some pretty wild parties.

Smiling to herself, the park ranger knew quite a few of the empty beer bottles were hers, as she had attend more than one party in the last few weeks up there. With Ryan gone, she now got to drive the surplus military combat mule by herself. The military mule was a small all-wheel-drive surplus military vehicle that had been donated to the parks department. Weighing only eight hundred pounds, the mule could transport well over a thousand pounds on its small flatbed. Ryan called it a door with four wheels, seat for one, and a sort of brake to help stop it. But this odd-looking powerful beast could climb just about anything the Esker could throw in front of it.

With the quick briefing finished, Tobin watched as the four officers knelt to start their slow crawl into the pitch black of the drains. Time was not on their side as the afternoon was getting late and sunset was not far away, but the real problem was the six o'clock high tide. With sea water already beginning to fill the salt marshes on the other side of the Esker, it would not be long until the Atlantic Ocean made its way into the storm drain again as it had done twice a day. The firefighter turned and climbed out of the ravine to go find Captain Hunt.

"OK, here we go!" Kim Sarfield called out to herself for confidence. She had not yet driven the all wheel drive machine by herself. Climbing into the driver's seat, the assistant park ranger put the keys into the ignition, and the military mule's gas engine immediately roared to life with a noisy clacking sound.

"Don't forget to buckle up," Kim said to herself in a mocking tone, imitating Gallagher. Reaching down to her waist, she forced the seat belt buckle into the clasp with a resounding *click*. "Off we go!" She shifted the mule into the forward gear.

"Captain, did you find something?" It had taken Tobin a few minutes to find Hunt. He had about given up and thought maybe the captain had gone home. Then he noticed some movement over near where Adam had disappeared.

"Not sure, Paul," the captain replied, rising to his feet and holding out something wrapped in a white handkerchief for the firefighter to see.

"What the heck did you find?" Looking down at the object, Tobin questioned, "You think this is what killed the boy? It looks like one of those seashells you hold up to your ear so you can hear the ocean inside." Noting some sort of tree branch about three feet in length that protruded from the top of the shell, he added, "Is the shell embedded on that stick?"

"Yes, it seems someone forced the stick into the top of the shell to use as a weapon," Hunt said as he examined the ragged edge of the shell. "This appears to be blood on the edges. You can see it where the shell cracked from some sort of impact."

"You thinking maybe Adam's head was the impact point?" Tobin asked, stunned by what he had just heard.

"I'm not sure, but it does seem we may have to consider it." Captain Hunt looked toward the Esker, as if feeling like something was watching them from the crest of the glacier.

"Police will be able to match this thing with the hole in the kid's baseball cap," Tobin spoke out as he waved a police officer to them. "Also the blood on the shell, to see if it matches Adam's."

"What ya need, Paul?" The police officer called out, quickening his pace toward the two firefighters in the high grass deep in right field.

"Captain Hunt thinks this stick and seashell may have something to do with the child's disappearance," he said, motioning to the object the captain held in his hand. "We need you to take this into evidence and transport it to the station for analysis."

Turning the object over a few times, the officer commented, "If this had anything to do with the boy's disappearance, I'm guessing this is more of a murder investigation now."

"You may be right, officer, but let's follow protocol and take this evidence to the station and get it processed as such," Tobin said, putting his hand on the officer's shoulder. "And I don't have to remind you that as evidence, this is not to be shown around first. It goes right to the station for processing."

"Will do, Paul. Transport to the station immediately." Glad for something to do, the officer turned and headed to his squad car.

Watching the officer climb into his squad car and drive off, Tobin looked toward the Esker, wondering what the hell was going on up there. "Well, Captain, I need to get back to the storm drain entrance and see what's going on with the teams inside the drains. What about you? It seems we have done everything we can, and now it's up to the police." Turning toward Hunt, Tobin saw he'd already started to walk away.

"I'm heading to the hospital to see how the park ranger is doing and give him a ride home if needed," Captain Hunt called out. Stopping for a moment, he added, "Paul, whatever is going on up on the Esker is dangerous, so please be careful. I do not want to lose anyone else to whatever this is." Not waiting for a response Hunt turned and headed for his truck for the drive to the hospital.

Tobin headed over to the storm drain to see how the police search mission was proceeding.

Maneuvering the mule was a bit tricky on the small trails that led up the side of the Esker. But once the assistant park ranger got to the top, she knew it would be easy driving on the tar and gravel. Most of the trashcans were located on the side of the road that ran the length of the Esker, and the ones that weren't were an easy task for the all-wheel-drive mule. Occasionally, teens would drag the barrels into the valley to collect trash and burn fires in the large steel cans for light as they partied into the early morning hours. Kim smiled, knowing just where the cans were as she had attended just such a party the other night with her new friend George Duff, maybe the toughest guy in Weymouth. George had been arrested numerous times for fighting and drinking. Kim liked the tough guy type. And she did like George with his wicked killer smile.

Reaching the top of the Esker, the assistant ranger stopped the machine for a moment to look down at the ball field where all of the commotion was still going on. "The kid is probably hiding at home," Kim said to herself, shaking her head, then she turned the machine to the left and headed toward her first trash can down by the Hingham Bridge. "Start at the end and work your way back," is what Ryan always said. And Ryan was the boss. The ranger gave the machine a bit of gas and started toward the Hingham Bridge on the rocky road.

"How are we doing down here?" Tobin called out as he climbed down into the ravine walking to where the two police officers and chief of police were peering into the b massive storm drain.

"Well, the first team finished up the left drain about ten minutes ago and found nothing," the police chief said, standing up to stretch. It had been a long hour of bending over the drain waiting for any news from the search teams. "The first team out of the storm drains reported nothing unusual, let alone any type of animal that could have attacked the park ranger."

Bending down to look into the storm drain, Tobin noticed a small, steady flow of salt water coming out of the drain. High tide was fast approaching now. "The men in there have much time, Chief. Tide is starting to come in and fill the drain," Tobin mentioned to the police chief.

"Coming out!" As if on cue, the two police officers who had been searching the right storm drain began climbing out.

"Did you find anything?" The police chief asked as he helped the three officers out of the drain.

"Nothing of interest to report in the right storm drains, Chief," the first officer called replied, stretching.

"Nothing? Are you sure? Tobin asked. "Did you find a doll at the end of the storm drain?"

"Nope," the first officer replied. "Got to the end and found the drain blocked by some sort of landslide."

"Paul, we did a thorough search of the right storm drain and found nothing," the second officer chimed in. "We did find the cave in as you described it, and we did a search for the doll all around the rock, but came up empty." He began climbing out of the ravine, then turned around. "Paul, I did hear children laughing and giggling, and it seemed to be coming from somewhere in the drains."

"Chief, I know what I saw and heard in there, and I did see that doll," the firefighter spoke out as he turned toward the police chief who was now also climbing out of the ravine.

Stopping at the top, the police chief turned back toward Tobin. "Son, I heard you, and frankly, I do believe everything you said about the attack, kids laughing, and the doll at the end of the storm drain. But whatever attacked you and the park ranger in the drains is not there now and neither is the doll. It seems we are at an end of this storm drain search matter."

Bending down, the firefighter took one last look into the blackness of the massive storm drain. No doll, no child, no creature that had attack him and the park ranger such a short time ago. Turning away from the storm drain, the firefighter began to climb out of the ravine. Then, hearing a child's laughter, he looked back as a small blue rubber ball bounced out of the drain.

Bending down, he picked it up and knew there was no reason to search the drains again. Whatever was in there was playing a game, it seemed. Maybe the ocean breeze had pushed the ball through the drains. Was it fear or exhaustion that kept the firefighter from heading back in? Turning back toward the ballpark, Tobin climbed out of the ravine and headed toward his car. It had been a long day.

"Mrs. Bertholdi, we did a thorough search of the storm drains under the Esker, and your son Adam was not there," the police chief spoke as he neared the child's mother and father. Father Gilday was standing nearby.

"Where is my child?" the confused mother cried out as she held onto her husband for much needed support and strength.

The police chief looked to Father Gilday for support.

MISSING RANGER

WAVING TO TWO CHILDREN on bikes, Assistant Park Ranger Kimberly Sarfield slowed the military mule to a crawl as the all terrain vehicle kicked up gravel off the Esker road.

"How are you doing today?" She called out to the kids who had stopped peddling to watch the strange machine go by.

"Great, Ranger," the two young boys called out as the odd looking vehicle slowly drove by.

Turning her attention back to the road, the park ranger started to step on the brakes as the vehicle was quickly gaining speed on the steep drop from the highest point on the Esker to one of the lowest points. She began to panic as the heavy vehicle gained speed rolling down the steep incline. Stepping on the brakes harder did little to stop the mule's forward motion. What had Ryan done when this happened? *What did Ryan do*? The ranger searched for answers, looking around at the few controls of the all-terrain vehicle.

"Now I remember," he said aloud over the roar of the mighty vehicle as it continued gaining speed. But it was too late. The high-pitched sound of the transmission screeched as the military mule lost control and darted toward the heavy brush on the right side of the tar and gravel road.

"Goddamn it!" Screaming out in terror, the assistant park ranger jammed the brake pedal with both feet. But the tiny vehicle was going too fast, and with no load of trash on board, the balloon tires just slid across the loose gravel road into the brush and trees.

Slamming into the underbrush, the mule continued accelerating into the thick underbrush and rolled down the steep incline into the thicker forest below. The sound of branches cracking filled the air as the park ranger screamed out.

Reaching for the seat belt, she tried to unbuckle herself but twenty years of rust on the snap refused to allow the buckle to unclasp. She screamed again in terror looking up at the huge tree that loomed directly ahead, then covered her face with her hands just as the vehicle hit.

Walking briskly into the main entrance of the emergency room, Captain Hunt noticed it was a slow day, as only a few people were sitting in the waiting room. The captain did not like hospitals very much and he hoped this visit to check on the ranger would be quick. The sterile smell was overwhelming and the bright lights made his eyes water as he stopped to let his eyes adjust to the bright glare.

"Hey there, Captain Hunt," A young woman called out immediately as he entered the main foyer of the emergency room.

Hunt turned to his neighbor's daughter, Margie McKay, who had grown up to become a nurse. "Margie, how are you doing today? Do you know where the park ranger is who came in a bit ago with an arm injury?"

"Sure do. He's in exam room four with Doctor Green. Should just be finishing up with him." The nurse motioned toward the exam room. "Kinda weird wound, don't ya think, Captain?" She added as the captain walked by her toward exam room four.

Stopping for a moment, Captain Hunt turned back toward the nurse. "How so?"

"Well, I was in there when Dr. Green pulled the object out of his arm." Stopping for a moment, she made sure no one else was around before continuing. "It was a saltwater mussel shell for sure, according to Dr. Green."

"Thanks, Margie. I'll keep that under my hat," Hunt quietly responded.

Stepping through the curtain and into the exam room, the captain found Ryan alone and pulling his shirt on over the injured arm that was heavily bandaged.

"How are you feeling, Ryan?" Hunt asked, reaching over to help the park ranger. The captain noticed the park ranger was wincing in pain as he pushed his arm into the sleeve.

"Good, Captain. Should be as good as new in a few weeks according to the doctor." Ryan tried to stand up, but a wave of nausea and dizziness struck the young park ranger.

Captain Hunt reached out to help steady him. "Easy there, Ryan. Sit back down for a bit to steady yourself."

"Thanks, Captain. The pain medication is stronger than I thought." Sitting back down on the exam table, the park ranger continued. "What was that thing in the storm drain, Captain Hunt?"

The captain's mind went back to the terror of years ago, in the darkness of the storm drains that ran under the Esker. How many nights had he laid awake late into the night? The pain and fear of that day was forever etched in the captain's mind. The fear of the attack that rendered his left hand nearly useless. The pain of a mutilated child's body being dragged into the darkness of the drain, never to be seen again. Yes, many painful nights.

"Captain Hunt, what attacked you that day under the Esker?" Regaining his composure, the ranger sat up on the exam table and waited for an answer.

Pausing for a moment as if trying to remember, Hunt turned toward the light shining through the window and slowly began to recall.

"We got a call about a missing child down around the Esker on Julia Road Park. When we arrived on the scene, it became clear very quickly that the child and a Weymouth police officer were somewhere in the storm drains."

"Excuse me, Captain Hunt," a pretty young nurse called out from the doorway. "Will you be taking the park ranger home today?" Handing a clip-board to the captain, she continued. "He's not allowed to drive for twelve hours due to the medication he was given for pain. Please sign here and here," she said, pointing.

"Well, I guess you're riding with me, Ryan." Captain Hunt handed the clip-board back to the nurse and headed out of the exam room. The ranger quickly followed, trying to keep up with the long gait of the captain.

"Hey, Captain, slow down a bit," Ryan called out as he swayed a bit. Grabbing the wall to steady himself, the ranger stopped for a moment.

Captain Hunt turned around. "Damn, Ryan, I'm sorry. I just hate being here." Walking quickly back, Hunt took Ryan by the arm to help steady him as they left the emergency room and moved into the fading afternoon sun. Captain Hunt continued his story of what had happened that day under the Esker.

"Like I said before, we got a call about a missing child maybe trapped under the Esker in the storm drains. When we pulled up to the scene, it was total chaos. A police officer had gone into the drain to find the child."

Interrupting the captain, the ranger asked, "Why didn't the police officer wait for you guys to attempt a search and rescue?"

Stopping on the passenger side of a bright red pickup truck, Captain Hunt said, "Here's my truck," helping the park ranger climb in. Slamming the door shut, the captain quickly moved around the truck and climbed into the driver's seat.

He continued his story. "Well, the officer heard the child screaming, according to the reports from the other officer on scene as well as several witness's, including the child's mother. Sergeant Giannone was a good friend of mine. We grew up together here in Weymouth."

The truck came to life and the captain reached over to turn the radio off. "Knowing Nick, Sergeant Giannone, he had to do something when that child started screaming." Looking to his left and then right, Captain Hunt moved slowly out of the parking lot and into the traffic, turning right onto Route 18 before going on.

"It started to rain the moment we entered Julia Road Park. Engine two arrived on scene a few minutes later. We didn't have much time. The rain was coming down harder, but more importantly, high tide was coming in, and at that point, the drains backflow with water from the Atlantic. The ocean water was already filling them when Tobin and I went into the storm drains."

"Do you know how many storm drains run under the Esker?" The park ranger asked when the captain paused for a moment.

"Well, hard to say, but according to the plans on file at the town hall, there are four entry tunnels on the marsh side of the Esker and just the one that opens into Julia Road Park on the town side." Captain Hunt pulled over, hearing the scream of a fire truck siren. "A few of the town's drains do connect to the storm drains under the Esker for rain overflow."

Looking over his shoulder, Captain Hunt pulled back out into the light traffic. "Not really sure how many miles there are, though, as most of the drain schematics were lost years ago." Then Hunt added, almost as an afterthought, "Heck, the Army Corps of Engineers put them in over thirty years ago. Weymouth was such a small place back then, I doubt anyone even gave it a second look at the time. Anyway, Paul had just entered the left drain, and I was about to follow when I caught a glimpse of movement in the right storm drain."

"Is that where you found the child? In the right storm drain?" The park ranger asked, already knowing the answer. But he could sense Captain Hunt was about to stop talking, and the ranger needed to know what the captain had battled.

"Yeah, about thirty yards in, I found the child." Shaking, with great sadness in his voice, Captain Hunt continued to describe the macabre scene like it had just happened instead of being eleven years before. "The child was sitting slumped over, his chin resting on his chest, shoulders hunched, like a broken toy. As I approached him, I could see he was dead. His shirt was ripped off and there was a slice into his belly. It appeared he'd been gutted by someone."

"Did you say someone or some*thing*, Captain?" Ryan questioned.

Nodding his head slowly, Captain Hunt continued. "I did say some*one*. This was not the work of an animal. This child had been cut open in a precise way with some sort of sharp object. Same thing with Officer Giannone. Whatever attacked him had peeled all the skin and hair off his head and was in the process of splitting his skull open with a clamshell when interrupted by Captain Hill and his rescue team."

"I'd never heard that either of those deaths were anything but a drowning," the park ranger remarked.

"Well, the town wouldn't announce that someone or something was disemboweling kids and cops under the Esker. And please, call me Butch; you've earned that after today," Hunt replied.

"Will do, Butch, but then you need to call me Ryan." The park ranger said before taking the conversation back to the thing in the storm drain. "Whatever attacked me was covered in seaweed and kinda shaped like a person from what I could see in the flashes of light." Pausing for a moment to see if Butch had heard him, Ryan waited to see if the captain would go on with his story.

Gathering his thoughts, Hunt began to describe what he had seen. "Well, I never really got a good look at it, but I would say it was like a big ball of seaweed when I punched out at it. Captain Hill, of the other rescue team that found Officer Giannone, also said the thing that attacked him was covered in seaweed and had large yellow eyes. I'm not sure what happened to the child after I was whacked wicked hard with something in the head. Doctors took pieces of seashell out of the wound on the top of my head. Glad Tobin was there to pull me out or I would have drowned or worse if that thing had come back for me." Butch rolled down his window to get some air as he was having trouble breathing after dredging up the memories. "That's about all I remember from that day under the Esker."

After a few deep breaths of the warm breeze, Captain asked, "Where do you live, Ryan?"

"Donnellan Circle, still with my parents," Ryan replied lazily, feeling the effects of the pain medication and a long day under the Esker. "I left my car down at the ranger station, though," Ryan added as an afterthought.

"It'll still be there tomorrow." Turning the truck on Donnellan Circle, Hunt was about to ask Ryan which house when Ryan pointed to a green one on the left.

"That's where I live, right there, in the green house with the garage."

Captain Hunt pulled into the driveway. "Do you need help into the house?"

"No, that's OK, I've got it, Butch."

After watching the park ranger climb the front stairs and go inside, Captain Hunt backed out of the driveway and headed home to ponder a long day at the Esker and the tragedy that had happened.

"Ugh, what the F?" Park Ranger Sarfield reached up to touch her forehead. The military mule had hit a large tree halfway down the marsh side of the Esker, slamming her head-first into the trunk. Thankfully, the rusted seat belt kept her from the full force of the impact.

Her own blood flowed freely down her face from the gash in her head. Pulling her hand back from the wound, the young park ranger began to panic as the late afternoon sun was vanishing behind the Esker. Reaching down, she fought to unbuckle herself with no luck the seat belt was locked tight.

The sound of movement nearby stopped her, and as the shadows of the forest deepened, the movement came closer. The sound of leaves rustling and faint sounds of children laughing echoed through the trees.

"Kids, is that you?" the park ranger called out, hoping the boys she had passed earlier were still around and had seen her accident. "Please, you two kids!" she screamed out as the kids' laughter continued to echo through the twilight that had descended upon the Esker.

Reaching down, Kimberly feverishly clawed at the rusted seat belt. The sounds of leaves rustling drew slowly closer to her. Something was coming up from the marshes down below the Esker. The sound of the children was close behind her. Struggling to turn around, she tried to catch sight of the children but it was too dark and the blood still flowing down her face hindered her vision.

A hideous animal like scream filled the night air in front of the military mule and she turned quickly toward the sound. But something grabbed the park ranger by her long red pony-tail and furiously began trying to pull her from the vehicle. Unable to fight back, the park ranger screamed in pain and terror.

Suddenly, the force from the thing pulling on her hair caused the seat belt buckle to snap, throwing the park ranger forward into whatever the creature was. For a moment, she was free of its grasp.

Groggy from the injury to her head, the park ranger struggled to get to her feet. The creature's hideous screams filled the cool night air once again. Kimberly turned quickly toward the top of the Esker, screaming again in fear as whatever it was grabbed her again, knocking her to the ground. She kicked back for another brief moment of freedom from the thing's grasp, but with blood freely flowing from her wound, she could feel herself slipping into unconsciousness even as she tried to claw her way back up the steep incline.

It was no use. Whatever had her was quickly back and starting to drag the park ranger back down the ravine toward the salt marshes at the edge of the Esker.

Grabbing at anything she could and struggling to get back on her feet, she screamed, "Please let me go, please let me go, please let me go! Dear God, please help me, please let me go, please let me go! Dear God, help me. Mother help me! Daddy, please help me! Daddy, help me, please!"

Whatever had her stopped for a moment, and Kimberly rolled onto her back and tried to wipe the blood from her eyes to see what had grabbed her. Looking up into the night sky, she saw that a full moon had risen, bathing the Esker in moon light. For a brief moment, she caught sight of something moving through the eerie gray glow of light in the forest canopy.

Crack! Something hit her in the head. She could feel her nose fracture and her teeth smash as the sound of children's laughter once again filled the night air. Fighting to stay conscious, the park ranger screamed out again. Whatever it was had started roughly dragging her again toward the marsh at the bottom of the Esker.

She could smell the salty mud and the sharp edges of sea grass cut her face and arms.

Then the soft mud of the marsh turned into cold concrete, and she realized she was being dragged into one of the storm drains that ran under the Esker. Reaching out, the park ranger grabbed for the side of the concrete drain to stop her movement and screamed in the type of terror that silenced the night, "*Help me, help me, please someone help me!*"

A swift tug from the creature, and the park ranger was pulled quickly into the blackness as her screams echoed through the saltwater marsh and the Esker before she was pulled deeper into the dark abyss. A bloody handprint on the concrete walls of the storm drain was the only message left by the young park ranger to say she was ever there.

WHALE ISLAND

"LET'S GET A MOVE on, Chris. I want to get to Whale Island while the tide is high enough to get close for some great bird pictures," the woman called out, climbing quickly out of the SUV.

Chris Childs followed, quickly helping his wife get the first of two kayaks off the racks on top of the truck.

It was turning out to be a beautiful July morning on the Esker, with a slight breeze rolling gently off the Atlantic Ocean as high tide started to reach its peak in the basin. The sun had started a lazy climb into the sky. There was not a ripple on the glass surface of the water. A seagull's screech off in the distance broke the silence of the moment. A picturesque morning on the Back River of the Esker.

Yes, it was also the perfect time to finally get near Whale Island and take a few pictures of the birds nesting there. A few of the woman's bird watcher friends had reported seeing an osprey flying over to the island. Now, that would be a great picture. *If true*, Ashland Childs thought with a grin as she helped her husband place the second kayak into the water at the south entrance to the Esker down by the Weymouth Dump. Yes, a front page picture of the osprey in the *Weymouth News*. If it was really there.

Grabbing her camera bag from the truck, Ashland pushed her kayak into the cool ocean water, climbing quickly into the sleek craft in one fluid motion. As she did so, she yelled over her right shoulder to her husband, "Last one to Whale Island is a Yankee fan.!"

"A Yankee fan can't have that," Chris called back as he watched his wife climb into the kayak. "Man, what a nice butt you have." He admired her sexy milky white butt spilling out of the skimpy bathing suit. Pushing his kayak into the still water of the Back River, Chris started to paddle to over take his wife in their friendly race to Whale Island.

"Why the rush, Ashland?" After a few powerful strokes of his paddle, he'd quickly caught up to his wife. He looked over at her long, flowing blonde hair hanging in a long ponytail out the back of her pink Boston Red Sox cap, her perfect ample breasts barely covered by her bikini top, and her deep tan from hours on the beach and kayaking. Yes, she was stunning and all his.

Slowing for a moment, Ashland called over to him, "We only have an hour or so before the tide starts pulling back out of the basin." Smiling at her husband, she continued, "After that, it will be wicked hard to paddle back to the launch point, and I want some strength left for fun in the woods when we get back. I brought our favorite blanket." Smiling a bit, she started to paddle ahead of her husband again.

"Well, let's get this done so we can get back," Chris called out, smiling a bit about what he called the guarantee blanket.

"I guess it was just dumb luck I packed a bottle of wine in with the lunch." Pushing the paddle deeper in-to water, he picked up the pace to catch up. The race was on.

After another ten minutes of brisk paddling and banter, Whale Island came into view. Located-about two hundred feet off the Esker and surround by mud marshes at low tide, the only easy way to get to the island was by boat at high tide. History says that when the Pilgrims left Plymouth on their way to Boston, they would camp on the island but stopped after a few trips where some of the Pilgrims disappeared in the night and were never found. The island was thought to be cursed and after that, was given a wide berth by travelers making their way to Boston.

Slowing to a drift, Ashland waited for Chris to drift up besides her. Looking toward Whale Island, she searched for any sign of birds nesting. Off to the left, there was movement a few feet in the undergrowth near the water. Ashland quickly brought the camera up to her eye and started to focus on the small island with the telephoto lens. Yes, there was something in the undergrowth on the left bank and it was pretty big. Hanging the camera around her neck, the woman could feel the excitement of what she was sure was the osprey, just waiting for her to snap a magnificent prize winning picture.

"OK, honey. I'll meet you around the other side in about thirty minutes," she called out as she began paddling slowly toward the left side of the island. "Be sure to take plenty of pictures and remember any good spots to show me on the way back," she added as she started to disappear around the inland side.

"Well, best do as the lady says. The sooner we are done, the sooner we get back to the blanket," Chris called out as his wife disappeared around the tip of Whale Island with a wave of her hand.

He started to move to the right side of the island to see if he could find any interesting birds to report back to his wife when they met up again.

Paddling slowly just a few feet from Whale Island, Ashland's strokes were almost invisible, dipping like a sharp knife into the still water. She didn't want to scare any birds that might be nesting or feeding in the brush near the water-line. There was some movement in the brush just a few feet ahead of her. Sure she had seen something hiding in the high grass about twenty feet ahead, she placed her paddle across the kayak.

Picking up her camera, she scanned the brush ahead with her telephoto lens. And yes, just ahead was the bird she had hoped to find. Pausing for a moment, she raised her camera again. Yes, it was an osprey nest with the mother in the nest unaware of her approach.

Quietly smiling a bit, she began to take pictures of the bird in rapid succession. Suddenly, the magnificent bird screamed out in surprise and terror, then quickly took flight from its nest. "Damn!" Ashland yelled as she quickly continued snapping photos. Arcing her camera, she followed the bird in flight, getting as many pictures as she could before the magnificent bird disappeared into the tree line of the Esker.

Sensing more than seeing movement in the sea grass surrounding the island, she turned to look. Whatever it was seemed to be coming nearer. A seagull screamed as it jumped into the air, startled by whatever was in the sea grass.

Something viciously grabbed the woman by her long pony-tail from behind the kayak. As it pulled her backward, her legs became tangled in the kayak. Ashland screamed in pain as she felt her back begin to crack from the force pulling her. Something grabbed her by the chin, muffling her screams as she fought to get her legs out of the kayak, and the smell of rotting flesh assaulted her senses when something slimy rubbed against her face.

A hideous scream from the creature filled the air. The attack on its defenseless prey continued, as it dragged the powerless woman out, tipping the kayak over in the process. The saltwater filled her mouth and lungs, muffling her scream. Struggling to the surface, Ashland fought to catch her breath and scream again. But it was no use as she felt a sharp crack to her head. Stunned from the blow, Ashland felt warm blood flow down her face and into her mouth. Reaching up to where she had been hit, she could feel a large gash in the back of her head ripping through a tear in her cap. Fighting off panic and trying to stay conscious, she started to cough out the sea water that was rapidly filling her lungs.

Trying again to scream, she was once again stuck with sharp object, this time on the side of her face. Her jaw went limp as the bone cracked, fractured by the relentless attack. Something again began to pull her under the salty water as she yelled in vain, pleading for her husband. "Christopher! Help!" But that was all she got out as the water covered her face again, and mercifully, Ashland began to black out as she was pulled deeper down into the blackness of the water.

Pausing for a moment, Chris started a slow drift in his kayak toward the end of Whale Island. Listening again to the stillness around him, he muttered, "I'm sure that was Ashland calling out. I bet she found the osprey she was hoping to get a few pictures of." Chris smiled as he started his slow paddle, watching the shoreline of the island for any bird signs. Not that he really cared, but his wife did, and in the end, that was all that really mattered. Reaching the end of the island, he saw an overturned kayak come slowly into view, floating in the current.

He knew the moment he saw it that it was hers and that it had been his wife calling out a moment ago. She must have gotten out onto the island and her kayak got away from her, he summarized as he pulled up next to the overturned craft. What else could have happened to her? She was an excellent swimmer and a lifeguard at Wessagusset Beach during the summer months. Her screams must have been her cursing the kayak.

Flipping the plastic boat over was easy and there was not much water in it, so it still floated. Tying it to the back of his own kayak, Chris called out to her. "Ashland! I have your kayak!" he yelled, paddling slowly around to where his wife had been exploring.

Continuing to paddle along the back side of the island, Chris again called out to his wife. "Ashland!" Not good; she should have answered by now. He steered his kayak toward an opening in the brush. The island was not that big, so she should have been able to hear and see him by then. Chris called out again, "Ashland! We need to get out of here soon before the tide gets too low." Pushing the paddle deeper into the water one last time, the tip of his kayak came to rest on the shore of Whale Island.

Grabbing hold of a low bush to steady him, Chris started to slowly climb out of the teetering kayak. Wouldn't seem fit for him to lose both of the kayaks. She would make the loss of both all his fault, he thought with a smile as he stepped onto the island and started to tie the crafts to the brush at the edge of the small beach.

Hearing some movements rapidly coming through the brush behind him, he started to turn to greet his wife. "Hey, honey, I found your kayak" he started to say before he was greeted with an intense pain in his right shoulder. Looking down, he screamed in pain as his knees startled to buckle.

He reached for the large stick that had gone through his shoulder. Something or someone had speared him. *"What the!"* the man began to scream out as something charged out of the dense brush, knocking the helpless man back into the water that surrounded Whale Island.

Trying to fight off whatever had attacked him, he pushed the creature away from him as they crashed back into the water, but it was no use. The creature was just lying on the helpless man, waiting for him to drown, it seemed. Pushing forward again, Chris could feel the pain of the spear through his now useless right shoulder, causing him to shriek in pain as the water began to fill his lungs. Reaching out one last time at the creature, he got hold of what he thought was seaweed and began to pull.

For a brief moment, the creature backed off, and Chris got his head above the water, but only for a moment. Whatever was attacking him was covered in seaweed. Catching a brief glimpse of the creature, he saw that it was big bigger than him and it was covered in seaweed to mask itself like camouflage.

The creature was panting heavily and seemed to be catching its breath as it glared down at its helpless prey. The sound of nervous giggling laughter of children filled the air behind the attacker, and a low snarl issued from the creature.

It slowly leaned forward, and grabbing the injured man by the back of his head, the creature attacked again, smashing something sharp into its prey's face over and over again. Chris raised his left hand to shield himself from the attack as the assault continued. Two more rapid hits to Chris's left arm, and he could feel the bones in his forearm shatter as it fell limply to his side.

The sound of excited children laughing and giggling continued. The helpless man tried to see where the sounds were coming from. With no defense left, Chris began to cry out his wife's name one last time. "Ashland!" But it was only a whisper, and as the creature forced his face beneath the cool waters, the man slipped into blackness. But suddenly, the creature grabbed Chris by the hair and pulled him out of the water and onto the slope of the island.

The pain was unbearable as the creature hauled Chris by the crude spear that went through his right shoulder and dragged him deeper into the thick brush on Whale Island. He tried to scream out in pain, but it was no use. Only the sound of gurgling blood and labored breathing came out.

Dragging Chris into a small clearing in the brush, the creature stopped and roughly slammed the spear that ran though his shoulder into the soft ground, leaving him helpless. The creature knew the prey was still alive but could go nowhere, and Chris knew he was at the mercy of this animal or whatever it was. Looking up into the trees, Chris watched as the clouds moved slowly through the sky. His mind started to wander to his beautiful wife; did she run into this creature also? Was she dead or alive? Wishing he had loved her more, wishing he had told her that he loved her more often, he cried out her name softly, "Ashland!" He looked to his left and started to scream out in anger and pain. The crude spear came out of the ground as he struggled to his feet. Chris had found his wife.

Hanging upside down, her feet roughly tied to a tree limb with vines, the body of Ashland Childs swung from the limb, her hands barely touching the ground. Her bathing suit had been ripped off. Was she alive? Chris hoped so as he called out her name. "Ashland?" Her back was toward him and her beautiful body swayed in the ocean breeze. Calling out his wife's name again, Chris began a slow painful crawl to his wife's side.

"Honey, I'm here," he called out, grabbing his wife's hand. Blood covered the ground and she was cold to the touch. Turning the body around, he wailed in fear, anger, and terror.

But the creature had returned with some sort of grunt and scream. It pounced onto the injured man's back and grabbed him by the hair.

Refusing to let go of his wife's hand, Chris screamed out again in pain as the creature had stabbed something into the dying husband's throat.

Feeling the darkness overcoming him, the husband knew it was over. Looking up at his beautiful Ashland, he whimpered. His wife had been cut open from the navel to the neck, and all of her organs were in a pile about five feet from her body; her beautiful face was a smashed mess. Holding his wife's hand tighter, the man whispered, "I love you," as the creature attacked him again.

TRASH ON THE ESKER

"RYAN, TIME TO GET up. Time to get up," his mother called up the stairs to his bedroom. "Ryan, you told me to make sure you were up by seven. Well, it's seven, so time to get up."

"Got it, Ma. I'm up," Ryan called out to his mother as he slowly slipped his feet over the side of the bed to the floor. Sitting up, the park ranger could feel throbbing in his injured arm.

"Your father picked up your medication last night as you asked. It's on the kitchen table. I'm heading off to work now. I left you breakfast," Ryan's mother called out before he heard the front door slam shut. A moment later, the car started and pulled quickly out of the driveway and headed up the street.

"Well, let's do this." Rising a bit too quickly, Ryan fell back onto the bed. The pain in his injured arm greeted him as he tried to use his injured arm to get out of bed. The second time worked better as Ryan used his other hand to push himself up and off the bed. Taking a few minutes, he got his clothes on and headed down-stairs for breakfast. Then he would be off to Esker Park for a fun day of working on a few new trails and trying to put the tragedy of yesterday behind him.

Sitting down at the kitchen table, Ryan looked over the breakfast his mother had left on the table for him. Cereal, toast, and orange juice. While he was eating, a voiced called in through the screen door on the back porch.

"Hey, Ryan, how are you feeling this morning? Eating is always a good sign."

Without turning around, Ryan called back to the firefighter he had spent yesterday with under the Esker, searching for the lost child. "Hey, Paul, how ya doing today?"

"Not feeling too bad considering yesterday and all that happened," Tobin replied, entering the kitchen.

Sitting down at the kitchen table, he continued. "Butch Hunt said you may need a ride to the Esker today."

"Yeah, I was planning on walking, but a ride would be appreciated." The park ranger finished the last of his cereal. "Well, daylight is wasting. I'm ready if you are."

Climbing into his truck, Tobin watched as the park ranger opened the other door and climbed slowly, then shut the door. Slamming the truck into gear, Paul started the quick five-minute drive to the park ranger station at the Elva Road entrances to the Esker.

"Paul, do you understand any of what happened yesterday?" Ryan asked. "Has Adam been found yet?" Turning to watch the traffic flow slowly down Green Street, the park ranger already knew the answer.

"No, he wasn't found last night and never returned home." Looking to his left, Paul turned onto Green then continued to Elva.

"I don't think this child will be found alive,"Ryan continued to talk, needing to understand all that had occurred. "Been in some bad spots the last few years, in 'Nam, but at least I knew what I was fighting."

"Never been in combat, Ryan, but I have tangled before with whatever those things are under the Esker," Paul replied. Slowing for a moment, he started the drive down the steep road to the Esker.

"Do you know what they are?" The park ranger questioned.

"Well, I'm pretty sure there are more than one of whatever attacked us yesterday. Back in 1964, Captain Hunt and I were one search and rescue team. Captain Hill and another firefighter were rescue team two. Both teams entered the drains at different points on the Esker, and both teams were attacked at the same time during the attempt to rescue the McGrath child and Officer Giannone." Pulling the truck to a stop next to the ranger station, the firefighter took a moment to gather his thoughts and continued.

"Whatever attacked us back in 1964 was covered in seaweed also, and according to both Hunt and Hill, whatever attacked them looked more human in form than a four legged animal. The newspapers speculated it was some sort of sea creature that got stuck in the drains during low tide. Both men were sure it human characteristics."

"Seems to make sense, not sure what attacked me yesterday, but it was quick and wasn't afraid of me, that's for sure. It seems to have the hunting skills of a man, the way it slashed me with something. An animal wouldn't make a weapon," the park ranger uttered thoughtfully as he opened the door to the pickup and climbed out.

The morning sun was already promising a warm day on the Esker. Better get things done early and head home early in the afternoon, Ryan thought as he slammed the door of the truck.

"Paul, where is Captain Hunt today?" the park ranger called out almost as an after-thought. "Maybe the three of us could get together and sketch this thing out with a time line and a rough idea of size and a few other things that might help figure out what we are dealing with in case we bump into it again."

"Not a bad idea; I'll ask him about it. Though if you're up on the Esker, you'll probably see him before me," Tobin replied as he looked toward the lush green hillside of the Esker.

"Really, why is that?" Paul asked, following his new friend's gaze toward the Esker, as if the creature was watching them from the safety of the hillside.

"Captain likes to fish on the Back River. He drives a twenty-eight foot all red Boston whaler fishing boat with the words Hunt One written on the back. Just give him a wave and he'll come in. Loves telling fish stories about the one that got away."

"I will do that. Thanks for the ride, Paul. See ya soon," Ryan called out as the pick-up drove off in a cloud of dust. Turning back toward the Esker, Ryan noticed Kimberly Sarfield's park ranger car was already in one of the parking spots next to the ranger station. Smiling a bit, he said to himself, "Early bird gets the worm."

He walked slowly up the few steps into the ranger station, and the phone started to ring as soon as he opens the door. Walking quickly to the phone, Ryan picked it up on the third ring. "Esker ranger station. May I help you?"

A frantic woman's voice quickly replied, "Yes. This is June Sarfield, Kim's mother. Is she there?"

"Mrs. Sarfield, this is Ryan Gallagher, the park ranger. I just got here, and Kim's car is parked outside." As he spoke, he looked out the window and noticed the garage door was open and one of the mules was missing. "I'm pretty sure Kim is up on the Esker collecting trash right now. I'll go find her and have her call you right away."

"Thank you, Ryan. She didn't come home last night. Her father and I are very worried; this isn't like her. We'll be waiting for her call."

Sensing a bit of relief in the frantic mother's voice, the ranger heard the phone hang up on the other end.

"Well, let's go find our missing ranger." Grabbing a pair of binoculars off his desk, Ryan headed out the door to fire up the other mule and starts looking for Kim.

The mule caught on the first turn of the key, and the small powerful engine screamed noisily to life. The *clack clack clack* of the motor hummed as the park ranger shifted the mule into gear and started toward the trail that led to the top of the Esker.

The trail to the fire road was steep but no match for the all-wheel-drive surplus military mule as the small vehicle scrambled up the steep inclines, at times with all four wheels spinning madly to gain grip on the trail. After a bumpy five-minute ride, the park ranger pulled the mule to a stop as he turned onto the fire road that ran along the top of the Esker.

"Which way did Kim go first?" Ryan mumbled to himself, turning to the right toward the first trash can stationed down by the Boy Scout Bridge. As he pushed the gas pedal down, the mule jumped forward for the ten-minute ride to the bridge down in the marshes that crossed a small water inlet to the other side, where the Esker met the Back River. It was early still, so thankfully, there were not many people around. A few joggers waved as they struggled to climb the incline, and the ranger stepped hard on the brakes to slow the mule's speed.

Ryan noticed an older couple walking their dog across the Boy Scout Bridge as the ranger pulled the noisy mule to a stop near the trash can off to the left.

"Morning, folks. How is the walk going this morning?" he called out as the older couple slowly crossed the wooden bridge toward the ranger.

Their dog, a very big German shepherd, walked closely with the couple. The dog was sizing the ranger up, making sure he was not a threat to them.

"Good morning, Ranger. Our daily walk is going just fine, as usual. Just wish the park was a bit cleaner," the woman called out as they approached the ranger. Motioning to the over-flowing trash can at the base of the bridge, she continued. "How can you let this happen to such a beautiful place as the Esker?"

"I can assure you, ma'am, this will not happen again. This trash can is supposed to be picked up daily. I'll make sure it gets taken care of today and every day after this," the ranger called out as he noticed something moving in the brush a few hundred feet past the bridge on the side the couple had just come from.

Shaking the man's hand as the couple climbed slowly down the log stairs from the bridge, Ryan asked, "Did you happen to see my assistant park ranger while you were walking over on that part of the Esker?" All the while, he was watching the brush where he had seen the movement.

The ranger was sure someone or something was watching or had been stalking the couple and their dog. The slight movement in the brush confirmed something was there and still watching the small group.

"No, sorry, we didn't see anyone. But we did see two kayaks tied up at Whale Island. My name is Ken Keller, and this is my wife Eliza. Our four-legged friend here is Leonidas," the man spoke as he patted the massive dog's head.

"That sure is a big good looking dog," Ryan replied. Reaching out to pat the dog's head, the ranger was surprised when the dog turned back toward the bridge and growled in a low, menacing tone at whatever was on the other side in the brush, right where the ranger had been looking moments before.

"Easy there, Leonidas. Easy," the man called out pulling the massive dog's leash a bit as he patted the dog's head. "We had to cut our walk short today as something was bothering Leonidas and we couldn't calm him down at all. We didn't see anything, but Leonidas was spooked."

The woman chipped in with a final word to the ranger. "We'd better not see this trash here tomorrow if you want to keep your job, Ranger."

Laughing a bit, the old man added, "Don't worry, Ranger. She doesn't mean it-just hates to see trash on the Esker." Looking toward his wife the man started to follow her up to the gravel road but stopped for a moment, turning back toward the Boy Scout Bridge. "We did hear what we thought sounded like calls for help or screaming from the water's edge. Looked but saw nothing; must have been some boaters or echoes, but it sure seemed real."

The park ranger looked again toward the spot where he was sure something was watching him from. The movement had seemed to stop. "Letting my imagination get the better of me," he said to himself. He headed across the bridge to check out the couple's report of two abandoned kayaks tied up at Whale Island.

A quick ten-minute walk along the trail brought the ranger to a high point on the trail that overlooked much of the Back River and gave him a great view of Whale Island about fifty yards away. From this vantage point, the ranger could see most of the island with his powerful binoculars. Scanning it for signs of the kayakers, the ranger was sure there was some movement on the island, but it was pretty much hidden by the dense brush of the island.

Scanning the waterline, the ranger could see the two kayaks clearly tied together almost at the middle of the island. Continuing to look along the shoreline of the island, he next saw what appeared to be a crudely made log raft held together with what looked like vines and salt grass. The raft looked about ten feet long and about half as wide and appeared to be pulled slightly onto the island so as not to drift away. "Hmmm, kids are getting smarter these days. A new place for smoking pot and drinking, I bet," the ranger yelled out, hoping to see a few teenagers stand up, knowing they'd been found.

Whatever was on the island stopped moving when he yelled out, but nothing else as the ranger continued to scan the island, hoping for an easy way of fixing this problem.

"I'll be out to Whale Island later today. Please do not let me find you there!" he called out again. *Kids,* the ranger thought to himself, realizing that just a few years ago, he had done the same thing. Turning back toward the Boy Scout Bridge, the ranger knew he still had a lost ranger to find and trash to empty before the end of the day.

Climbing back into the mule, the ranger figured Kim must be at the other end of the Esker, down by the drive-in theater near the Hingham

Bridge. Turning one last time, the ranger looked back to where he had seen something earlier. Whatever was there was gone now, but the ranger could feel something watching him from the salt marsh off to his left. "It's just my Vietnam paranoia," the ranger said to himself. But that paranoia had saved his life more than once, and he had learned to respect that feeling. Hitting the gas on the mule, Ryan started the bumpy ride to the other end of the Esker.

THREE MISSING ON THE ESKER

SLOWING THE MULE TO a stop, the ranger neared the steep decline just above Holmes Avenue. Two young boys on bikes were waving at him as they walked their bikes up the steep incline of the hill. Not too many folks without gears on their bikes could make it up, but the ride down was always fun. Thinking back to the days when the ranger and his friends used to do just that, way back in their youth, he smiled. "Sorry, mister. We thought you were the ranger," one of the young boys said as they stopped next to the mule.

"Have you seen her up on the Esker today?" Ryan asked the boys.

"No. We went down to the Hingham Bridge and back."

"Was the lady ranger riding one of these?" Ryan asked.

The boys nodded.

"When and where did you see her?" Ryan questioned.

"We saw her right here yesterday," the first boy said.

"Yeah, she waved as she drove by yesterday morning, but we haven't seen anyone today," one of the boys replied.

"Wait, you've been down to the Hingham Bridge today? Did you see if the trash cans down there had been emptied lately?" Ryan asked, hoping the answer was yes.

"Nah, they were all overflowing with trash. We were there yesterday, too, and they were still wicked full," the older boy called out as the boys started to climb on their bikes and ride off. "We need to get home, Ranger, or Mom will kill us," he added as they slowly rode off.

"Well, this day is not getting any better," Ryan mumbled softly as he scanned the Esker for any sign of the missing ranger. Kim Sarfield was known among the locals as a party person. She loved drinking, smoking weed, and just plain partying. Normally, the ranger would just write this off as the young girl sleeping it off at one of her friend's houses. But given what had been going on the last few days, he knew he needed to find the woman quickly.

Climbing off the mule, he grabbed his binoculars and walked to the edge of the road to stretch his legs and scan the marshes on the Back River side of the Esker. As Ryan walked to the edge of the road, he could see the brush to his left had been trampled and broken down.

Yes, it appeared something had gone off the road there and traveled down into the valley, the ranger thought as he bent down to examine the broken foliage. It was the mule that made the tracks; the imprints of the large wheels were obvious in the soft ground. "Damn, Kim must have driven off the road here," Ryan said as he stood and started down the steep incline.

"Kim, it's me, Ryan!" the ranger called out as he grabbed a tree to slow his descent down the steep incline.

"Kim, are you down here?" called out again. The park ranger stopped for a moment to catch his breath. Ryan could make out the mule about hundred-feet down in the valley, very close to the bottom and the salt marshes. The morning sun was just beginning to penetrate the lush covering of the trees, giving the ranger a better picture of what must have happen.

Approaching the mule from the rear of the vehicle, Ryan could see that Sarfield was not in the mule. But he could tell she had been in it for the ride down into the valley. Moving slowly around to the front of the vehicle, he noticed the seat belt had been torn off. There was blood on the tree where Kim must have struck her head when the mule hit. Bits of her blonde hair were firmly stuck in the tree from the impact.

"This is not good," Ryan spoke out as he continued the search for signs of where Kim may have gone after the crash. Off to the left of the mule, the ranger found more blood on the ground. Had Kim stumbled off the mule and fallen there after the accident? The bush was badly crushed and it appeared there may have been a struggle. A bloodied rock lay off to the side. Had Kim hit her head during the ride down into the valley? He called out her name again. "Kim, where are you?"

Standing up, Ryan noticed the crushed leaves and ground continued down into the salt marsh. Grabbing hold of some trees the ranger started to follow the trail, stepping out into the marsh a few minutes later where the trail ended at the water. High tide was in, and the Atlantic Ocean rose right up to the edge of the Esker.

"Ryan!" a voice called out from beyond the marsh.

It was Captain Hunt in his bright yellow boat, moving slowly toward the Esker. The captain skillfully brought the boat to a halt. "Can only do this at high tide, Butch called out as the boat came to a smooth stop. So Ryan, what's up?" Hunt asked as the ranger walked quickly toward the boat.

"Got a missing ranger, Captain. Kim Sarfield; been missing since yesterday morning." Turning toward the Esker, Ryan continued as he pointed at the tree line. "Found her mule halfway down the embankment, all smashed up and blood in a few places."

"No sign of Kim anywhere?" Butch asked, climbing out of the boat and walking a few feet to the tree line. "Show me where you found the mule Ryan."

Turning quickly around, the park ranger walked a few feet down the marsh and into the tree line with Captain Hunt close behind.

The sounds of the Esker were everywhere as the two men climbed up the steep incline to the tree where the mule had made an abrupt stop on its way down.

Walking slowly around the vehicle, Hunt struggled to maintain his balance. Glancing up at the Esker, he could clearly see the trail the mule left as the vehicle plummeted. "Must have been quite a ride," the captain spoke, examining the tree where the mule had stopped. Strands of long blonde hair showed where Kim's head had made impact with the tree during the crash.

"It looks like she got out and fell to the ground over here," Ryan called out, kneeling to examine a small pool of blood.

"No. Kim was attacked and pulled out of the mule." Turning the seat belt over, Hunt could see the clasp had been broken by some violent force.

"Maybe the belt broke from the impact," Ryan called back, standing. The ranger was sure something was watching them from the shadows above and to their right.

"I doubt it, Ryan. The force of the break says otherwise. Like something grabbed her from behind and pulled," Hunt said, turning to look where the park ranger was staring.

"What makes you so sure?" Ryan asked, taking a few steps up the incline to get a better look into the shadows.

"Many years of accident reconstruction shows me what happened here," Captain Hunt said as he walked over to where Ryan had found the blood a few moments earlier. Dropping down to one knee, he could see the faint out-line of a body in the leaves and moist ground. "Seems she fell here and then was dragged that way." Rising, Hunt started to slowly follow the drag marks down the Esker to the marsh.

Taking one last look up, Ryan turned and quickly followed the captain.

Stepping out into the sunlight, Captain Hunt paused for a moment for his eyes to adjust to the brightness of the noon sun. "Yes, Kim was dragged out here. Of that, I am sure." Hunt began to realize that Kim Sarfield would never be found alive, if at all.

"How can you be sure, Butch?" Stepping out into the light, Ryan looked down at where the captain was kneeling.

"I taught tracking for a number of years to a group of Boy Scouts." Standing up, Hunt continued to follow the trail for about another ten feet, where it disappeared into the cool waters of the Back River. "But there is your real problem, Ryan," he called out, pointing to an object just under the surface of the water.

Stepping forward, Ryan looked to where the captain was pointing. "Damn, this just turned deadly." Under the water was a storm drain entrance that would be uncovered when the tide was low.

"You think Kim was dragged in there last night when the tide was out?" He took a few steps forward until the water started to lap on the ranger's boots.

"Yes, that is exactly what I think. And whatever this thing is that is attacking people has picked up its pace the last few days." Captain Hunt turned and quickly strode toward his boat a few feet down the shoreline.

Following quickly behind, the park ranger called out, "Butch, we need to close the Esker."

"Way ahead of you, Ryan." Picking up the radio microphone in the boat, Captain Hunt called out, "Station one, station=one, Captain Hunt calling Over." Pausing for a moment, the captain repeated the call.

On the second attempt, a familiar voice answered. "Station one receiving, Captain Hunt. Over." It was Tobin.

"Paul, I'm up here on the Esker with Ryan." Pausing for a moment, the captain looked toward the Esker where there was movement just inside the dense woods. "Paul, we have a missing ranger up here, Kim Sarfield from the signs we've found; she may be hurt. Over." Continuing to watch the woods, he saw the movement had stopped or backed deeper in.

"Roger that, Captain Hunt. We also have a report of a possible multiple drowning down by Whale Island."

Pausing for a moment, Hunt motioned for the park ranger to get onto the boat with a sweeping motion of his hand. "Paul, did you say drowning down at Whale Island?" the captain answered.

"Roger that. Some hikers have reported two empty kayaks floating in the Reversing Falls area and an SUV down at the Puritan Road entrance to the Esker. The SUV belongs to Chris and Ashland Childs."

"Roger that. Paul, the ranger and I will check out the Whale Island area and see if we can come up with something." Captain Hunt=started the boat's powerful twin one hundred=fifty Mercury outboards roared into life. "Paul, get the police to start closing the Esker. We'll get back to you after we check out Whale Island." Dropping the microphone, Captain Hunt threw both throttles forward, and the powerful Boston whaler leaped almost out of the water, knocking the park ranger back into one of the seats.

CLOSE THE ESKER

THE WHALER CUT QUICKLY through the glass like ocean as Captain Hunt kept the throttles pegged to maximum power, and the twin Mercury one=hundred fifty horsepower outboards screamed out in joyful pain. The sounds of the powerful motors made conversation impossible between the two men on the speeding boat. But talk was not needed at this point as both men knew deep down this was no drowning and neither of the Childs would be found.

After a few minutes, Hunt began to slow the boat, calling out as he did, "The Reversing Falls Peninsula." He pointed to a small land mass jutting out from the Esker. "Just after the bend, that is Whale Island." The ranger was now standing as the boat slowed to a crawl.

"Here we go," Hunt said, bringing the Boston whaler to a slow stop on the calm Back River. Whale Island was fifty yards away.

Picking up the binoculars around his neck, the ranger did a quick scan of the island. "Nothing moving on the island, Butch. I do see two kayaks tied near the Reversing Falls side earlier today, I saw some sort of log raft near the north end of the island, but it seems to be gone." Ryan lowered the binoculars.

"Captain Hunt, this is Lieutenant Tobin. Over," the boat radio squawked, breaking the silence over the water.

"Go ahead, Paul. This is Butch. Over."

Pushing the throttles slowly forward Hunt moved toward Whale Island and said to the ranger, "We need to be quick, Ryan. We have maybe thirty minutes before we need to leave as the tide is starting to go out."

Tobin's voice came over the radio. "Yes, the police have station cars at the three entrances and are warning folks to travel in groups on the Esker. Over."

"Did you tell them I said they needed to close the park? Over." Captain Hunt responded as he pulled back the throttles to idle on the boat.

"Sure did, Butch. The police chief said two things to your request. Over."

"What did he say? Over."

"Only a selectman can close down the park; a private citizen can not. Over."

"Thanks, Paul. Did you have any more news on the Childs? Over." Motioning to the park ranger to tie the boat to a tree, Captain Hunt handed the ranger the tie rope from the boat.

"Yes. Their SUV is at the Weymouth Dump entrance. Family says they were trying to get a few pictures of the osprey that are nesting on Whale Island. They left about seven o'clock this morning. Over."

"Thanks, Paul. We're at Whale Island now. We'll let you know if we find anything. Over." Dropping the microphone, Captain Hunt followed the ranger out of the boat and onto Whale Island.

Walking over to the kayaks, the ranger noticed blood covered both of the small crafts. "Take a look at this, Butch." Kneeling down, Ryan could see a struggle had taken place, and fresh blood could be seen spattered on the ground.

"The blood seems to lead inland." Looking over the ranger's shoulder, Captain Hunt turned and gazed into the thick brush that covered the island.

"Well, let's take a look and see what we find." Slapping the ranger's shoulder, Hunt started slowly walking into the bushes.

"There used to be a yacht club here on Whale Island back in the early nineteen= hundreds." Stopping for a moment, the captain continued to push the brush aside as he stepped into a clearing in the center of the island.

"Dear God, Butch, what happened here?" Ryan called out as he stepped up next to Captain Hunt.

Hunt heard the question, but could not speak. What appeared to be human remains littered the ground. Pieces of flesh and human organs were stacked in a pile at the edge of the clearing. In the center of all the carnage, two feet cut off just above the ankles hung tied from a tree limb by vines and sea grass. Blood still dripped slowly from the severed feet, flowing into a growing pool on the ground.

"I don't think the Childs drowned, Ryan." Moving slowly into the clearing, Captain Hunt reached down and picked up a camera. "Maybe there will be something on this camera we can use to see what happened here. He slowly started to back away. This carnage would be forever etched in his mind, and memories of the McGrath boy flowed rapidly back. Whatever had done this might still be lurking just beyond their vision in the thick underbrush on the other side of the clearing.

"Come on, Ryan. This is a crime scene; we need to report this," Hunt said.

Taking one more quick look around, Ryan was sure he heard the faint laughter of children from the other side of the clearing before he turned to follow the captain back to the boat.

"Fire station one. Fire station one. Come in, please. Over." Watching the ranger climb into the boat the, captain was sure something was slowly moving toward them in the thick brush, perhaps sizing the two men up for an attack.

"Ryan, quick, tie the two kayaks to the back of my boat," the captain called out as he watched the ranger grab the front kayak line and pull the two crafts toward the boat. Watching the ranger tie the kayaks to his boat, the captain called out again.

"Ryan, cast off. We need to get out of here before the tide goes out and grounds us." The captain could see the water around the boat was getting very shallow. They may already have stayed too long.

"Station one. Go, Butch. Over." The sound of the radio crackling had made whatever was moving toward them stop for a moment. The beep, beep, beep sound of the twin outboards lowering into the water echoed around them.

"Ryan, push off quick with that oar," the captain called out turning the keys. The outboards roared to life.

Turning the boat slowly as he backed away from Whale Island, Captain Hunt breathed a sigh of relief. "Ryan, scan the island again with the binoculars. I'm sure something was moving toward us as we cast off."

"Butch, what did you find on the island? Over." The radio again crackled to life as Paul waited for a report.

Picking up the microphone, Hunt radioed back. "Paul, meet us down at the Weymouth Dump entrance with the police chief in ten minutes. Over."

Reaching down, Ryan quickly grabbed the binoculars and started to scan Whale Island. "Got something, Butch!" he advised, pointing toward the clearing they had just left moments ago.

"What have you got Ryan?" Bringing the powerful motors too idle, the fire chief turned to look where the park ranger was pointing.

"Got movement in the clearing. Can't be sure. It appears to be human in form but it keeps ducking into the underbrush." The park ranger continued to scan the island. "Can you get closer, Butch? It might be the thing we're looking for."

The fire chief could see the water was quickly receding, and the tops of the salt grass were beginning to show. "No dice, Ryan. We need to back out even more or we'll get grounded." Looking off toward the horizon, Butch could see storm clouds rapidly moving down the Back River, and the ominous clouds meant rain was not far away. "We need to move it, Ryan. We have storms moving in." Pushing the throttles forward, Hunt urged the Boston whaler slowly away from the island. He took one more quick glance toward the island before turning the boat toward the Weymouth Dump entrance.

"Well, whatever is there needs to stay there until the tide comes back in!" Ryan called out as the powerful boat roared down the Back River toward the dump.

The ride to the dump entrance took five minutes, during which the noise from the motors made talking impossible. Both men tried to grasp what they had just seen on Whale Island. Rounding the bend of the Esker just past the Puritan Road entrance, the Weymouth town dump came into view about a hundred yards away. As they neared the sandy boat ramp, Hunt could see quite a crowd had gathered. There were maybe twenty or more people gathered at the water's edge to see what was going on. Off to the side of the crowd stood the solitary figure of Father Gilday.

Captain Hunt shut the boat's motors off and the boat slowly glided toward the crowd at the edge of the water. Climbing out, the park ranger and Captain Hunt were overwhelmed with questions from the anxious crowd.

"Captain Hunt, did you find my daughter and her husband?" Ashland Childs's mother asked.

"Sorry, Becky. We did a thorough search of Whale Island, but there was no sign of them."

"But you have their kayaks tied up behind your boat," the distraught mother called out, pointing at the kayaks as if the captain did not know they were there.

"I know. We found them tied up on the island." Pausing for a moment, the captain then continued. "We searched the island and found no evidence that your daughter or her husband were there."

"You said the boats were tied up on the island?" a voice in the crowd called out.

"Yes, but again, we did not find the couple on the island," Hunt advised to the anxious crowd.

"Butch, Ryan, over here!"

Looking toward the sound of the voice, both men could see Paul, Police Chief Bob Smollett, and Selectman Bob Rober standing off to the side of the growing crowd.

Hunt and the ranger quickly moved over to the waiting Weymouth officials.

"Your message from the boat didn't say much, Butch," Paul said, reaching out for the captain's hand. "Hey, Ryan. How is the arm feeling?"

Nodding to the other gentleman in the small crowd, Butch knew everyone was waiting to hear what they had found on Whale Island. "Chief, it seems from what the ranger and I saw on the island, there was a brutal murder at some point today over there."

The police chief had known Captain Hunt for many years, and though they did not always get along, Smollett knew the captain stuck to facts. "Damn, Butch, do you know who or how?"

Watching the crowd starting to move a bit toward the town officials, Hunt knew he needed to keep his voice down. "When the ranger and I got to the island, we found ripped flesh and a pile of what appeared to be human organs in the clearing."

"How do you know it wasn't just some hunter cleaning his fresh kill and gutting fish?" Selectman Bob Rober queried.

The captain replied, "We also found what appeared to be two severed feet hanging from a branch and some torn clothing in a pile near the organs and flesh."

The group of town officials were stunned and stared in disbelief as Hunt continued speaking. "Ryan and I did not examine any more of the island or wander into the crime scene. Whatever did this may still be on Whale Island, as we were pretty sure something was watching us as we left Whale island."

"Yeah, whatever was there, I caught a glimpse of it as we backed away," The park ranger chimed in.

"Did you see what it was, Ryan?" Paul asked.

Pausing, the ranger needed to think about what he'd really seen in the brush just minutes ago. "It's hard to say. It did appear to be a man of some sort, but he stayed hunched over in the brush, so I can't say for sure. Whatever it was knew we were watching, so it stayed concealed itself in the brush."

Nodding in agreement, Captain Hunt continued, "Whatever it was seemed to be sizing us up. It didn't seem to be scared of us, that's for sure. I think it might have attacked us had we stayed on the island any longer."

"I think we need to have the harbor master position a patrol boat off Whale Island until we can get back on the island," Selectman Rober said as Police Chief Smollett nodded in agreement. Turning toward his car, Smollett went to make the call to the harbor master using the police radio.

"Well, the tide will be back in tonight, then we can get a few men onto the island and see if we can piece together what happened," Rober continued as he watched the police chief come back to the small group.

"OK, the harbor master is sending out a patrol craft that will stand watch over Whale Island until we can get back on it at high tide tonight," the police chief said, looking toward the black clouds moving down the Back River as the first few rain drops began to fall.

"Where is my daughter?!" Becky Wisdom screamed at the small group of men. Turning, they could see the distraught mother had made her way from the larger crowd to the small group of town officials.

"Butch Hunt, we've known each other since we were kid," the distraught mother continued, coming face to face with the retired firefighter. Now you tell me what has you so scared on Whale Island that you can not tell a mother about her child."

"Becky, I'm not sure what happened on the island. You've got to believe that," Hunt spoke softly to the pleading mother.

"God damn it, Butch. Is my daughter on the island? If you don't tell me, I will crawl to that island if I have to right now and find out for myself."

A quiet hush fell over the small crowd of onlookers. A sea-gull screamed off in the distance and the sound echoed over the river, and thunder clapped as the rain began to fall.

Butch Hunt looked at the mother. "Yes, Becky. I do believe your daughter and her husband are on Whale Island."

"Dear God, Butch, what are you saying? Why did you leave them there? Go get my child for me, please!" she screamed, falling into the out stretched arms of Father Gilday.

As the rain began to fall harder, the priest began a quiet prayer that only the sobbing woman could hear.

> *He will wipe every tear from their eyes.*
> *There will be no more death or mourning or crying or*
> *pain, for the old order of things has passed away.*

Turning away from the crying woman, the park ranger walked to the edge of the Back River. Off in the distance, the Weymouth harbor master's boat had arrived on scene just off of Whale Island and begun its lonely picket duty of the island. The flashing lights of the boat cast an eerie glow on the water, and its powerful searchlight tried in vain to light the island as the rain continued its murderous downpour.

"Ryan, what did you see on Whale Island that's got you so quiet?" Hunched over from the steady downpour, Paul stood near the park ranger and watched as the patrol boat moved slowly along the Back River.

Pausing for a moment, the ranger gathered his thoughts. "I saw some messed up stuff in' Nam, but what Butch and I saw today is the stuff nightmares are made of."

"Paul, Ryan, come over here please!" Captain Hunt's voice boomed over the storm. Turning around, the two young men headed over to where Hunt was standing with the police chief a few feet away, next to the chief's car.

"What's up, Butch?" Paul asked as the two men neared the police car. Looking around, Paul could see only Father Gilday and the mother still nearby. Everyone else had headed back to their cars and home to get out of the driving rain.

"The chief here wants to use my boat to help get a team on the island as soon as possible. I agree with him, and I want you two to be part of the team that goes. You, Paul, in case someone gets hurt. Your EMT training you would be a great help. And, Ryan, as the head park ranger for the Esker, you need to be there also."

"I'll have three fully armed officers on the island for protection, if need be," the police chief yelled over the downpour. Looking toward the Back River for a moment, he then continued. "Your job is simple enough, secure Whale Island. Make sure there are no threats there. After that, we can get a state investigation team in to figure out what happened there."

"Be back here at eight tonight. The tide will be coming back in and will be high enough around ten. At that time, I'll land the five of you on Whale Island," Hunt yelled out. Turning toward his boat, the retired fire chief knew it would be a long wait to get back on the island.

"Butch, what has happened to my daughter?!" The scream of desperation stopped the retired firefighter in his tracks.

Turning toward the woman and the priest, Hunt took a few quick steps toward them. Reaching out and taking the woman's hands, he said, "Becky, I don't know what happened to her or even if she is still on the island. But I promise you I will find out tonight. I promise you that."

The distraught mother gave a small nod as she turned her head into Father Gilday's shoulder and they walked away toward the priest's car.

"Police Chief Smollett, do you have a moment?" the park ranger called out, walking quickly toward the police chief's car.

"Yes, ranger what is it?" Climbing into the police car, the chief rolled the window down as the park ranger approached.

"I still have a missing ranger. Kim Sarfield is up here on the Esker. I found her vehicle down in the ravine near the drive In," Ryan explained, bending down to talk to the chief.

"Kim Sarfield you said? Right, Ranger?" The chief turned the ignition and the engine roared to life. "Don't worry about Kim. That girl has run away more times than I can count. Lately, she just does not go home after a long night of drinking."

"But her parents called me today and said she hasn't been home in two days," Ryan replied, stepping back from the police car.

"Tell Mrs. Sarfield if she is worried to fill out a police report. She knows how; she does them often, but the girl always shows up at some point," the police chief said, then he drove away in the steady downpour.

REZ PARTY

"HEY GEORGE, HOW ARE you today?" Knowing full well it was not the voice of his girl-friend, Kim Sarfield, George Duff turned slowly around, his killer smile all set to charm. George knew that voice. It was Bonnie, the Easy Dream, as she was called in school.

"Hey, Bonnie, how are you today?" His smile was in full effect; the rest was easy. "Are you going to the Rez party tonight? I was planning on going, but it seems Kim isn't, so I don't want to go alone." Looking around Bicknell Square, George kept the smile going, looking around as if expecting Kim to show up at any moment and ruin his plans.

"I bet she went on another drinking bender and is too scared to show her zit covered face." Bonnie's hatred for Kim was obvious as the sarcasm dripped. She moved a bit closer to him. "Besides, George, if Kim can't take care of her man, what good is she?"

Smiling a bit more, George knew he had Bonnie tonight, with her dark skin from a long summer of beach tanning, long black hair, a nice rack, and such a sweet face. "Yes, guess you're right, Bonnie. Let's meet in the Burger King parking lot at, say, eight o'clock. I'll get the beer and pot. Let's have some fun tonight up on the Rez."

"See you then at eight, Burger King parking lot," Bonnie called out as she and her two friends walked quickly away.

"Rez party tonight? Ya know, George, if Kim finds out, she'll kick Bonnie's ass," Wally called out, watching the girls walk away.

Smiling a bit, George turned to his friend who had stood quietly by as he and Bonnie had talked. "I'm counting on it. It'll be fun to have a wicked girl fight at the party. Yes, there is a Rez party, now a party of four down in the valley."

Looking at his watch, Wally said, "Well, we better get moving. It's six o'clock now; not much time to buy beer, get a few joints, and get cleaned up." He watched the girls cross Bridge Street and disappear behind the drug store.

Before George could answer his friend, a voice in a slow moving car called out, "Excuse me. Excuse me, George, have you seen Kim today?" George had seen the sporty gray Chevy Camaro parked in the Bicknell School parking lot for the last hour. It was Kim's mother.

"Hey, Mrs. Sarfield. How are you today?" he asked, as the car came to a slow stop. George could see where Kim got her body. Mrs. Sarfield was dressed in a halter top and very short shorts, her long blonde hair covering her huge breasts. "I would love to nail this mother," George whispered to Wally as they approached the car.

The smell of beer wafted from the car as the two young men leaned in to get a better look at Kim's mother in the front seat. The rumor was she loved her men young, and her daughter had lost more than one of her boyfriends to her mother over the years.

"Sorry, I haven't seen Kim in the last three or four days," George replied, staring at the older woman as she sat in her car.

She turned to show more of her scantily clad breasts to the young men. Kim's mother loved to tease her daughter's boyfriends. "She hasn't been home since she went to work three days ago. She hasn't even called me or any of her friends," Kim's mother replied, taking a long swig from the bottle of beer that was nestled between her thighs.

"I swear that daughter of mine will be the death of me."

"Have you checked with the ranger down at the Esker?" Wally chipped in, hopeful the older lady would notice him, but she kept her eyes on her daughter's boyfriend, George.

"So, do you have any idea where Kim could be?" Reaching up, the woman touched the young man's hand, softly moving her fingers back and forth.

"Like I said, Mrs. Sarfield, I haven't seen Kim in the last three or four days," he mumbled as he relished the feel of her mother's fingers on his hand. *Wow, Kim's mother is hitting on me,* he thought, feeling an erection starting in his tight fitting jeans from the soft caresses.

"I've heard from some of Kim's friends that you and her were partying a few nights ago on the Esker, I mean the Rez. Well, if you do see her, please bring her home tonight. And if you don't, please come by and tell me so," she said, pulling her hand away from his. "Either way, drop by later tonight and maybe we can figure out together where she." Kim's mother put the car into drive and slowly pulled away. With a wave of her hand, she steered the gray Camaro onto Bridge Street, then she hit the gas, causing the tires to screech.

"It would seem, George, you have a busy night tonight," Wally called out as he headed away. "See you back at Burger King around eight." Wally disappeared behind the Weymouth Bank and headed home to get ready for the Rez party for four, or if Kim showed up, a night at the fights.

"Where is Kim? George quietly asked himself as he turned and headed for home to shower and change.

Their last night of drinking on the Rez had gone well enough, and afterward, in Kim's car up on Great Hill Park, they smoked and drank a lot. The sex was great; Kim knew her stuff in the back seat. But her whole "Do you love me?" thing was getting old. Heck, they had only been dating a few months and already, the crazy broad was talking about love. Yes, it was time to dump Kim and move on to Bonnie.

There was still beer to get and hide over by the drive-in theater. The pot was easy enough. There were still a few joints at home from the last pound he was selling. *Time to party,* George thought as he headed down Green Street to his house.

"Bonnie, you know if Kim finds out you're meeting George tonight, she'll kick your ass badly," Tina said as she hugged her friend in the Burger King parking lot. Bonnie always loved Tina, and her curly long blonde hair that hung down to her butt was to die for. "What time are you meeting him?" Tina asked. Looking around the lot, Tina could see it was full of cars, but no kids were about. Most Rez parties started here with the kids gathering and then heading up onto the Esker as a group.

"George said he and Wally would meet us here around eight. And besides, Tina, nothing is going to happen. Even if it does, it's not my problem if Kim can't keep her man happy." Bonnie looked into the car mirror, adjusting her halter top to give maximum exposure of her deeply tanned breasts.

"Just the same, Bonnie, you're looking for a beating from Kim. Remember how badly she beat up Ann Kay a few parties ago just because Ann talked with George?"

"I'm not worried. No one has even seen that slut for the last week, and if she does show her face at the Rez party, I'll kick her ass good." Lighting a joint, Bonnie continued. "Besides, George doesn't want her anymore; he wants me now." Bonnie took a hit of the joint and passed it to Tina.

Tina took a long hit, knowing her friend was talking trash. In all the fights Tina had seen Kim Sarfield in, never once did Kim even come close to losing. Most times, Kim beat the other girl unconscious and bloody. Kim had a mean streak, that was for sure. If Bonnie expected any help from her if Kim showed up, she was mistaken. Tina passed the joint back to Bonnie.

"Hey, Tina. Hey, Bonnie. Are you ready for a fun drunken high night?" Laughing a bit, Wally walked up to the girls. "Have you seen George yet?" he asked as he took the joint from Bonnie.

"Hey, Wally. Nope, not a sign of George. Beginning to think he's blowing me off." Taking the joint from the young man, Bonnie continued. "Maybe Kim showed up and he's taking her to the Rez party."

Letting the thick gray smoke escape from his lungs, Wally continued, "Nah, Kim's mother showed up in Bicknell Square a few hours ago looking for her. She told George and me that Kim hasn't been home for three or four days now."

Tina smiled a bit at Wally, inhaling a long hit on the joint, her small breasts pushing at the flimsy fabric of her white shirt.

"Three or four days? Wow, that's a long time, even for Kim. Does anyone know where she is?" Bonnie continued to scan the parking lot, looking for George. "I guess George isn't showing up tonight," she concluded.

"Sure he is, Bonnie. I bet he got stuck buying the beer. He'll be here soon; he's wicked excited about hanging with you tonight," Wally said, taking the joint from Bonnie. "Here he comes now. Wally pointed to the far side of the lot as George came out of the trees over by the Weymouth drive-in.

Trotting quickly over to his three friends, George took the joint from Wally. The smell of beer was already heavy on George's breath, and from the glow in his eyes, this was not his first joint today. "Hey, girls. What's up, Wally? George said, the tip of the joint glowing a bright orange as the young man took a long hit, almost finishing it.

"George, where have you been?" Moving toward her date for the night, Bonnie continued with her questioning. "Were you with Kim? Is that why you were late? I'm no one's seconds; get that straight," the young woman spoke angrily.

"Don't worry, baby. I was just hiding the beer over in the woods." Putting his arm around Bonnie and pulling her tight, George kissed her. "Is that better, baby? Come on; we have a party to go to."

"How are we going to get into the Rez? The police have all the exits closed because someone is missing up there," Tina mentioned as she moved closer to Wally.

"Don't worry, Tina. We'll just sneak in through the drive-in side." Putting his arm around Tina, Wally gave his date for the night a quick kiss. "The cops are fat and lazy and will just sit in their cars by the entrances," Wally added, kissing Tina again.

"Yeah, it's getting late. I don't want to miss any of the party. Let's grab the beer," George called out, taking Bonnie's hand. The group started toward the woods where George had stashed the beer.

Lighting another joint, George inhaled deeply. The wave of nirvana was over-coming him. Passing the joint to Wally, George smiled a bit. "We're in for a great night," he whispered to his friend as they headed into the woods of the Rez.

The walk to the valley where the party was to take place took the better part of an hour. There was no moon out that night due to the rain clouds in the sky, making the four kids walk in darkness. Only the light from the streets below the Esker gave them what they needed to navigate the black gravel road that ran along the top of the Esker.

The police were easy to get by as they were stationed only at the entrances to the park. The rain had been off and on all day, and the cops spent most of the time in their squad cars.

"I can see my house from here," Tina called out, pointing down at Hinston Road. "See? The fourth house from the end of the road. That's my house."

"Yeah, we see it, Tina. So after the party, we have the shortest route home. I told my mother I was staying with you tonight," Bonnie called out. She turned to George. "Hey, baby. What are you looking at?" The group of four kids were at the highest point of the Esker and could see most of it from this vantage point.

"Over there by Whale Island, there are a couple of police boats. See the blue flashing lights on the water?" George said as the lights of the police boats flashed over the Back River. "They have a few spotlights shining on the island."

"Yah, who cares? We're going down there, and I guess we aren't the only ones' partying tonight on the Rez."

Looking to where his friend Wally was pointing, George began to smile. Down in the valley was a raging bonfire and around the fire was a lot of movement. The sounds of screaming and yelling drifted up from the valley below.

"Times is wasting; let's go," Bonnie called out as she started down the steep trail.

Following Bonnie, George grinned as he watched the sexy lady in front of him, her sweet butt swaying in her tight jeans. Turning around, George called out to his friend. "Hey, come on you two; party time!" But Wally and Tina were not there. The six-pack of beer Wally had been carrying was on the ground where the couple had been standing moments ago.

Laughing a bit, George mumbled to himself, "Go get her, Wally Not wasting any time tonight."

Turning, George continued to follow Bonnie down into the ravine where the raging bonfire and party was. As he stepped into the clearing, George yelled, "Party time; I'm here!"

Grabbing him by the arm as he entered the clearing, Bonnie looked over her shoulder. "George, where are Tina and Wally?"

"I guess they thought four was a drag and went off by themselves for a bit." Popping a beer and taking a long drink, he added, "Don't worry, Bonnie. They'll be around sooner or later. Tina is safe with Wally. Let's party." Taking Bonnie by the hand, George started to walk toward the raging fire.

"That's strange…no one is here," Bonnie said as they neared the fire. "We could hear and see lots of people from up on the road, but now everyone is gone."

"Don't worry, whoever started the fire will be back. Until then, let's get high." Sitting on a log close to the fire, George gave Bonnie a smile, and with a wave of his hand, the girl rushed into his arms.

"Thanks, Wally. I didn't want to tell Bonnie that I'm leaving tonight for California." Lighting a joint, Tina took a hit and passed it to Wally, who walked over to sit with the pretty girl on a park bench just off the trail leading down to the ravine.

"Does anybody else know you're going to California, Tina?" Taking the joint from the pretty blonde, Wally knew his chances of scoring were getting slim.

"No, and I don't know anyone in California, either. I just know it's time to go anywhere else. I can't stay here anymore." Tina started to cry softly as she continued. "I'm not sure where I belong, but I do think my dreams are out there in California. Maybe my music career will catch on out there."

"California is pretty far away, Tina. Heck, it's almost on the other side of the county," Wally said with a smile, putting his arm around her. "But you gotta chase your dreams wherever they may be, Tina."

"True enough, Wally. I need to go soon. My bus leaves at midnight from the Grey-hound station in Boston." Standing up, Tina began to cry. "I need to go, Wally. Tell everyone I said good-bye."

Wally knew his chances of scoring were gone, and also, one of the prettiest girls he knew and a good friend was leaving Weymouth, maybe for good. "Take care, Tina. You'll be missed. Do you want me to walk you down the hill?"

"No. I'll be fine; my stuff is all packed. Just need to grab it and get to Quincy and head into Boston." Reaching over, Tina gave Wally an easy kiss on the lips, then turned and walked away into the darkness of the Esker.

Finishing the joint, Wally thought about what had just happened. Staggering to his feet, feeling the buzz, he muttered, "Better find George and that party. I may still score yet." Picking up the beers from where he had left them, Wally started to stagger down the steep trail that led down into the valley.

Stumbling into the opening of the valley floor, Wally called out, "George, where are you?" Pausing for a moment, the young teen realized there was no one in the valley. Walking closer to the raging fire, he mumbled to himself, "Great party. I'm here by myself. George and Bonnie must have taken off already. But who started the fire?"

The pot and alcohol had taken effect, and he sat down on a log near the fire to sort things out. But it was no use. After a few minutes, Wally opened another beer. "Great. Friends leaving me alone on the Rez." Turning to his left, Wally was sure he heard the sound of rustling brush. "Great, you're back, George!" Wally called out as he started toward the sounds that was coming closer.

Crack, crack, crack. The sound of gunfire filled the night air, and the screams of men and sirens of police boats on the Back River wailed. The whir of a low flying helicopter filled the air. Turning toward the noise, Wally took several quick steps to the edge of the salt marsh to get a better look at what was happening over on Whale Island. The sounds of gunfire continued. The police patrol boats were moving quickly around to the Esker side of Whale Island, their lights flashing toward it. The rain had started again, not hard enough to penetrate the thick tree covering of the valley, but out on the Back River, the rain was making it tough to see what was happening just a hundred yards away, where Wally stood at the edge of the salt marsh.

"George, come here quick! You've gotta see this!" Wally called out to his friend as he sensed someone was moving closer to him from the clearing. Suddenly, a loud scream of pain came from Whale Island and something or someone broke through the brush of the island, falling or jumping into the Back River. Two men followed the creature to the edge of the island as they continued shooting toward where the creature had landed and disappeared under the dark waters of the Back river. The two police boats raced around the island to the splash point. "Wow, did you see that George?"

Crack! The pain was intense as something hit Wally in the head from behind and his knees started to buckle. Wally tried to move away from a second blow that caught his right shoulder. He wasn't sure if it was because of the pot, but neither hit really hurt. The young teenager knew he was in trouble. The steady stream of blood now running down his face obscured his vision. The warm metallic taste of blood filled his mouth.

Why was George hitting him he wondered, as the teen screamed out his friend's name. "George, stop hitting me!" But turning to face his friend, Wally quickly realized it wasn't George. *Crack!* Another blow to the teen's face. Taking a step back, Wally tripped over his own feet and fell to the ground.

The sound of kids laughing filled the air somewhere behind the blaze of the fire. Slowly pulling himself up to a kneeling position, Wally wiped the blood from his eyes. Trying to focus on the blur in front of him, he screamed out in pain as the creature was once again upon him. The sounds of the creature's attack echoed through the valley and over the marsh.

TERROR ISLAND

TURNING ONTO PURITAN ROAD, Paul glanced down at the clock radio on the truck dash-board. Ten minutes to eight. It would not do to be late. Captain Hunt was big one punctuality. But if the carnage on Whale Island was as Butch and Ryan said, tonight might be a good time to be late. Slowing down, Paul waved and slowly made his way past the police car that blocked the entrance to Esker Park. Blue lights flashing in the rainy mist, the officer rolled down his window and waved the firefighter past the road block.

Turning slowly onto the tar and gravel fire road, the firefighter drove another few minutes until he came to the boat ramp down by the town dump. Pulling his truck next to several other vehicles, he parked and walked over to where Ryan and Hunt were standing by the captain's boat at the water's edge. "Hey, Ryan, Butch. All ready for a trip to Terror Island?" Paul asked as Captain Hunt reached out and shook his hand.

"Seems about the right name for where we're going," Ryan said, holding out his hand to shake Tobin's hand.

"OK, well the police special forces are here." Captain Hunt motion as three heavily armed police officers walked toward the men near the water's edge.

"Hey, Butch, fun night for a boat ride of terror on the Back River," one of the officers called out. "I hear you saw some hairy stuff on the island. Want to fill me in?"

Butch reach out and shook hands with Bob Hastery, long time Weymouth resident and head of the Weymouth Police Special Operations Unit for the last five years. "Hey, Bob. I'd like you to meet Park Ranger Ryan Gallagher, and you know Paul."

"Hey, Paul. Nice to meet you, Ryan. So, Butch, what did you see on Whale Island? Or more importantly, what didn't you see that got you spooked?"

"You read my report about what we saw on our search of the clearing in the center of the island. Ryan and I were sure something or someone was in the bushes watching us as we searched. We didn't move forward as we were not carrying any weapons or knew what we could be up against. So we got off the island and had Chief Smollett station patrol boats around it to make sure whatever it is stays there."

Looking out over the water, Captain Hunt could see a second Weymouth police boat had joined the first both were now on patrol all around the island.

"Looks like the tide is coming in pretty quick tonight. Must be the storm pushing it in quicker than usual," Hunt commented to no one in particular. "Should be able to get to Whale Island in the next hour or so."

Opening a folder, Captain Hunt pulled out a picture and passed it to the police officer. "We found a camera on the island that's been identified as Ashland Child's by her mother Becky. Most of the pictures were of the osprey that's living there. But this one picture may be something," he said, handing the picture to the police officer.

After scanning the photo, the police officer passed it to the other two officers to look at. He commented, "It seems to be something covered in seaweed in the background of the picture. You can see the eyes are yellowish in color. The blurriness suggests it is moving toward the camera. So it seems whatever is on the island understands camouflage techniques. This is good to know. Thanks, Butch. All right, men, let's make sure our equipment is ready. Don't want any mistakes with this thing." Bob Hastery motioned to the other two police officers, who moved off to check their equipment one more time before heading to the island.

"So, Butch, how do you want to approach this?" Hastery said, walking up next to the retired fire chief. "I read your report about what happened in the storm drains years ago. You talked about a creature covered in seaweed and yellow eyes. Do you think this is the same creature from 1964?"

"Well, this is your game, Bob. I'm just the taxi, but let's say we land on the north side of the island where Ryan and I started and you and your men move across the island slowly. As for the creature, beats me. It's hard to think this thing could have stayed hidden all these years up here on the Esker."

"Seems like an easy enough plan. We can cover the island in ten minutes to make sure there are no threats. If there is a threat, it'll be driven to the far side of the island and the patrol boats can fight whatever it is or we'll capture or kill it." Smiling a bit, the police offer turned and went with his men to prepare for the search of Whale Island.

"So, Butch, what do you want Ryan and me to do while the police do their thing?" Paul asked as he took a few steps toward the slow waves touching the shoreline.

"Well, follow the police onto the island and render assistance as needed or not. Hopefully, your services will not be needed. But I'm thinking the whole thing could get nasty pretty quick if that thing is still on Whale Island."

"You think it's still there?" Ryan asked as he came to stand next to the two men. Silently, all three men stared out at the island as if whatever they were talking about might show itself. The sounds of the powerful patrol boats engines rumbled quietly over the water, their blue lights casting an eerie glow onto Whale Island.

"Well, I'm pretty sure whatever it is could swim off the island by now, even with the patrol boats out there. But it could not have taken its kill with it, that's for sure. So yes, I am guessing this thing would wait it out to keep its kill." Shuddering a bit the cool night breeze, Captain Hunt realized the gravity of what he had just said. That thing was still on the island and waiting for them.

"Let's get this show on the water," the lead police officer called out as the three officers walked over to the boat and began putting their equipment into the front of the large Boston whaler. "Butch, when we get out there, let's do a slow circle of the island. I'll get the patrol boats to light up the island with their searchlights as we move around it. After the second pass, we'll land where you suggested."

Nodding in agreement, Captain Hunt climbed into his boat and the five other men began to push it into the water and then climb in as the boat floated freely in the calm waters of the back river.

Beep, beep, beep, echoed in the night over the marsh as the twin outboards lowered. "Please be seated, gentlemen," Captain Hunt called out, turning the keys the powerful outboards came to life.

"Harbor patrol boats, this is Search One. We are on our way to the island, ETA-three minutes. Light it up, please." Clicking off the microphone attached to his vest, the lead officer smiled a bit. "Get me out there, Butch. Let's go." Holding onto the back of Butch's seat, the grinned as Butch hit the throttles of the powerful boat. Back River came alive as the two Weymouth Harbor Patrol boats turned their powerful spotlights onto Whale Island.

The sounds of the police sirens on the two patrol boats was ear splitting, Paul thought as he held onto the boat as they raced toward Whale Island. Off in the distance, on the Esker, the young firefighter saw a raging bonfire in the valley by Hinston Road. *As soon as we slow down, I need to report that fire. Bet the kids are partying tonight,* the firefighter thought to himself as they neared the island.

The powerful spotlights had turned the island into daylight as the radio crackled. "We have movement on Whale Island! I repeat, we have movement on Whale Island!" the excited voice of one of the patrol boats captains called out over the radio.

Racing past the island on the outward side, Captain Hunt threw the boat into a hard left turn. Then, backing off the throttles, the powerful boat quickly began to slow down. The three officers knelt on the left side, their automatic weapons pointed at the island. The patrol boats had shut down their sirens but kept their lights trained on the island. The rain had started again as Hunt's boat neared the far end of the island. Turning left again, the captain called out, "One minute until we land the boat; be ready. Paul, Ryan, look sharp. As we land on the island, get out and steady the boat for the officers!"

"State Air One. State Air One, we are ready to search Whale Island. Over!" the lead officer called into the microphone on his vest. Butch knew State Air One was the call sign for a Massachusetts State Police helicopter, so one must be in the area.

"Roger. State Air One inbound, ETA one minute!" came the call back over the radio. Already the *chop, chop, chop* sound of the powerful Bell helicopter could be heard, and it seemed to Ryan the helicopter was flying low and fast down the Back River from the Hingham Bridge entrance.

"OK, Butch, let's do this. Men, to the front of the boat; let's go!" the lead officer called out as Butch turned the powerful boat one last time and headed for the small sandy beach where he and Ryan had been just a few short hours ago.

The sound of the helicopter was almost overhead as the boat touched the beach and came to an abrupt halt. Ryan and Paul quickly jumped out along with the first of the three police officer. *Crack!* The first officer fell backward into the water as something struck him. The next officer off the boat opened fire into the brush where the attack appeared to have come from. The automatic weapon ripped into the underbrush as the officer moved forward. The third officer jumped off the boat and quickly followed the second officer into the dense underbrush, disappearing from the sight of the boat crew.

"Paul, get to the officer in the water!" Captain Hunt screamed, but the firefighter was already on it. Jumping into the cold water, Tobin grabbed the police officer and was already pulling him onto the small sandy beach of the island. "Ryan, follow the officers; they may need your help," Hunt called out.

Nodding in agreement, the park ranger quickly started toward the gunfire and screams on the far side of Whale Island.

The patrol boats had turned on their sirens again and raced toward the commotion. The gun-fire continued as the helicopter stationed itself over the center of the island, its powerful search light turning the macabre nighttime scene into a grizzly daylight. Screams and yelling filled the air as the crack of gunfire continued.

The rain was falling faster now. Climbing out of the boat, Butch knew the officer down was his old friend Bob Hastery. "Paul, how is he?" Hoping for the best but fearing the worst, Butch approached the area where the firefighter knelt over Hastery's body his old friend.

Breaking through the brush, Ryan slipped and fell into the center clearing of the island. The sound of gunfire was just a few feet away now.

Rising to his knees, Ryan watched as another officer fell to the ground after being struck by something. The last officer screamed out, firing into the brush on the far side of the island. On his feet again, Ryan raced through the clearing to the downed officer. The last officer standing was moving into the brush with his pistol drawn as he had used all the ammunition for his automatic weapon.

Grabbing the downed officer's microphone from his vest, Ryan called out, *"Two officers down! Repeat, two officers down on Whale Island! We need assistance out here."*

"Confirm call. Two officers down on Whale Island," was the smooth reply from police dispatch. "Officers down. Location Whale Island. Repeat, officers down. Location Whale Island. Weymouth Harbor Patrol respond."

Turning the officer over, the park ranger nearly vomited when he saw the officer's face had been split open by some sort of seashell. Ryan knew the officer was dead and there was nothing he could do at the moment. Vietnam was starting to haunt him; this was a fire fight. Picking up the officer's pistol, Ryan started to follow the last officer into the underbrush.

Crack, crack, crack the sound of the last officer's pistol being fired in rapid action could be heard as the patrol boats lit up the far side of the island. A hideous scream-pierced the air as whatever the officer was shooting at got hit. Suddenly, a creature bolted through the underbrush right into the park ranger, knocking him to the ground. The creature slowed for a moment, and then resumed its flight through the underbrush to the other side of the island.

Following in fast pursuit was the last officer, firing his pistol at the fleeing creature. Screams again filled the night air as the creature was again hit. Breaking through the brush on the far side of the island, the creature jumped into the Back River and disappeared under the dark water. The last officer and Ryan followed quickly to the water's edge, firing their weapons until both clips were empty.

Turning off their sirens, the harbor master boats started a slow patrol of the area where the creature had made it into the water. The helicopter called over the radio, "We are running low on fuel; returning to base."

Watching the helicopter switch off its searchlight and start to move off, Captain Hunt knew this mission was a total disaster. Two dead officers and the creature got away, or maybe it was dead at the bottom of the Back River. Either way, whatever was going on here on the Esker was not resolved that night.

Covering the dead officer's chest and face with his jacket, Paul was close to tears. Of course he had seen death before, but not like this. The officer had been hit in the neck with some sort of wooden spear.

Kneeling next to the body, Captain Hunt began to cry.

"Thirty years with the Weymouth Police; thirty years. Only to be murdered by whatever that thing was." Continuing to mumble to himself, Butch stumbled over to where the creature had jumped into the river and screamed, *"Thirty years, only to die like this? The McGrath boy, and so many more. I swear, if you're not dead, I will see you in hell. I swear I will put you in hell myself the next time we meet!"*

"I think we killed it, Butch. The officers and I must have shot that thing a dozen times judging from the amount of blood around here. It'll float to the surface soon and then we will know." Coming to stand next to the captain, the park ranger looked into the dark waters and beyond to the salt marsh. "Yes, Butch. I am sure we killed it."

Ahhh! a scream erupted from the Esker basin, where the bonfire still burned.

After a moment, the hideous sound of the creature could be heard. *Wahhh!*

Walking slowly to the water's edge, Ryan now knew this night would not be the last one of terror for the Esker. The creature's scream tore through him like a great shard of glass. He felt his eyes widen, pulse quicken, and heart thudding like a rock rattling in a box. The scream came again, angry, defiant, not human. The blood drained from Ryan's face, and before he was even aware of making a conscious decision, his legs were pounding furiously on the uneven muddy marsh track, his ears straining for more sounds, more clues as to where it had come from. Stopping next to the small group of men, he realized the sound had come from the bonfire off in the distance, where the Rez party was. "Butch we need to get over there now! If that thing made it to shore, there's no telling the damage it could do to a bunch of drunk and high kids!"

Reacting to the sound Butch quickly headed for his boat. Grabbing the radio mic, the captain spoke quickly, "Dispatch we have an incident on the Esker; the valley off Hinston Road. Please respond police, then ambulances and firefighters; hostility is highly probable. Repeat, hostility is highly probable. The park ranger and I are heading there now."

Dropping the mic as he climbed into the boat, Butch called out, "Come on, Ryan. Let's get over there. Paul, you stay with the officer and continue to secure the island. Be careful! You don't know if that thing will be back or if there are more lurking around!"

Pushing the boat away from the island, Ryan held on as Captain Hunt moved the throttles forward and headed toward the bonfire raging in the Esker valley.

INTO THE VALLEY

BECKY WATERS WAS SITTING in her patrol car at the Puritan Road entrance to Esker Park. Boring duty, but it was overtime. Simple enough; tell people the park was closed for the next few days. With the rain, the job was very easy. An older couple with a dog were her only disappointed people tonight. The officer was sure some of the local teens had gotten by the roadblock, but there were so many ways into the park, they could not all be patrolled. But the night was about to get busy as the police radio broke the silence of the night.

"Car forty eight, respond to disturbance in woods Hinston Road area, Esker Park Valley. Be advised, may be a hostile situation. Backup is being dispatched. Proceed with extreme caution." The voice of the female dispatcher was cool and precise.

"Car forty-eight responding to disturbance. Estimate backup time responding?" Not wanting to shoot the wrong person, Officer Waters waited for the reply from the police dispatch center.

"Be advised backup is ten minutes out. Captain Hunt and park ranger on scene moving into the area from Back River in a boat." The dispatcher continued with her call for additional units to the area. Esker Park was about to get busy. "Engine two, respond to scene. Ambulance unit three, respond to scene. Police units five, seven, and nine, report to scene, code three."

"This has got to do with whatever is happening out on Whale Island," Officer Waters mumbled to herself, climbing out of her police car and walking around to the trunk. "Better take old Betsy with me, just in case." Opening the trunk, the officer pulled out a pump-action shotgun, then Officer Waters started toward the Esker.

Hinston Road was a quick five-minute walk up a fairly steep incline. About halfway up was a trail that led down to the basin near the marshes. Off in the distance, the sound of responding units filled the night air. The smart move was to wait for backup. But Officer Waters needed to make a name for herself if she was going to make sergeant anytime soon. "It will be quicker if I enter the marsh here instead of climbing up to the top and coming back down into the basin," the eager officer summarized. Walking off the gravel road, she began to slowly enter the edge of the marsh.

Moving the boat closer to the shoreline, Captain Hunt could see movement just outside the light of the bonfire. "Ryan, I see movement just beyond the fire. Do you see it?" Hunt called out, slowing the boat as it neared the shoreline.

The park ranger crouched at the front of the boat as it neared the soft marsh grass of the Esker. Ryan was not going to be surprised by anything as they landed, like what happened on Whale Island. Being lazy and not on your game will get you dead in a moment like this.

It was like landing in a hot LZ all over again for the Vietnam veteran. The ranger could feel his heart pounding as he held his pistol out in a firing position while the boat came to a slow stop on the edge of the marsh grass. "I see it, Butch. Eyes on it!" Stepping quickly off the boat, Ryan moved rapidly to his right, pistol out in front of him. Moving behind a tree, the park ranger stopped and scanned the area where the movement was just beyond the glare of the bonfire.

From the boat, Captain Hunt watched as the park ranger moved from the boat to the tree. The basin was empty; no partying teens or any indication there had been a party at all that night on the Esker. Whatever was moving had stopped, and the retired fire chief could feel the cold gaze of something just beyond the glow of the bonfire. Off to his left, Hunt noticed one of the police patrol boats had moved into position, lights off, but it was there nevertheless.

"Come on, Paul, let's finish securing the island." The officer who was still alive on Whale Island began to move back toward the center of the island, calling for the fire-fighter to follow him into the brush. "I'm sure the island is secure. Nothing could have lived through that firefight," he said, almost reassuring himself. The officer continued into the clearing. "Damn, this is a mess," he muttered, moving slowly into the clearing and shining the flashlight slowly back and forth over the dead officer and the human remains littering the area.

Stepping slowly into the clearing, Tobin moved through the human remains carefully so as not to step on anything. The powerful flashlight lit up the pile of remains over to the left of the clearing. Lifting the light, the firefighter groaned. "Dear God, what would do this to a person?" Turning toward the firefighter's light, the police officer came forward to examine what was being illuminated.

"A hunter would do this," the officer said examining a pair of feet cut off at the ankles and tied to a branch of a tree. "It is easier to clean the kill hanging it upside down so the blood runs out of the carcass. We need to back out of here; this area is secure. Time to get some help out and find out what happened here." Motioning to Paul, the police officer started to back out of the clearing and they made their way back to the small beach to wait for help.

Grabbing the microphone, Hunt quietly called the patrol boat that was slowly drifting just off to his left. "Weymouth Harbor Patrol One." The cackle of the radio call drifted over the calmness of the Back River.

"Harbor One. Over," the call came back as the boat continued its slow drift on the calm waters.

"Harbor One. This is Captain Hunt. Park ranger is on the scene. Could you light up the area north of bonfire about fifteen yards. We have movement in that area." He watched the vague movement just beyond the fire that appeared to be slowly moving away from the fire, trying to not be seen.

Moving slowly along the edge of the salt marsh, Officer Waters continued heading toward the bonfire at the far edge of a clearing, her feet sinking slightly into the gray mud as she walked. Slapping at a mosquito that was biting her neck, the officer stopped as the sound of children's laughter could faintly be heard coming from the dense dark underbrush just ahead of her. The laughter was of younger children, not teenagers, the officer thought as she moved closer to the brush and laughter of the children.

"Kids, you need to come out. It is too late for you to be up on the Esker," Officer Waters quietly called out to the movement in the brush. "Kids," she whispered, a little louder this time. The sound of children's laughter continued for a moment. Pausing for a moment to get her bearing in the darkness, the officer slowly began to move into the underbrush, where the laughter of the children seemed to be coming from a short distance away, slightly off to the left...

Suddenly the Esker basin got very busy as the patrol boat switched on its powerful searchlights. "Waaahh!" the creature screamed out in anger as the powerful lights turned the Esker basin into daylight. *Whoop whoop whoop!* the siren on the patrol rang out in response to the creature's anger.

"What the!" Officer Waters yelled out, moving quickly forward into the underbrush. Things were getting out of hand quickly, and the officer needed to find the children that were hiding in the bush just a few feet from her. "There you are!" the officer called out as her powerful flashlight lit up three children all huddle in a small clearing in the brush.

Something was wrong here; the kids looked more like animals covered in mud and seaweed. The bright blue eyes of the three children glared menacingly back at Officer Waters. Suddenly, "AAaiiee! AAaiiee!" one of the children began to scream out in terror.

"Easy, kids. I am not going to hurt you!" Officer Waters called out, stepping forward into the clearing. She began to kneel to comfort the children.

Whack. The officer fell backwards as something of great force hit her and knocked her to the ground. The officer's bulletproof vest had taken the brunt of the hit, but the wind had been knocked out of her.

"Object is on the move! Repeat, object is on the move!" crackled over the police radio from the harbor patrol boat as its powerful engines rumbled into life. The boat began to move slowly, following the creature with the boat's powerful searchlights as the creature moved quickly from tree to tree across the basin toward the marsh.

Crack, crack! The sound of gunfire echoed from the patrol boat as one of the officers opened fire on the fleeing creature. The blue lights of approaching police cars were now on the service road on top of the Esker. The sound of a helicopter was drawing nearer.

"This creature is about to be caught," the park ranger mumbled to himself as he moved quickly forward, trying to catch a glimpse of the creature as it attempted to dodge the search light moving from tree to tree.

From Whale Island, Paul and the officer watched helplessly as the chase unfolded less than one hundred yards away from where they stood. The sound of gunfire continued from the patrol boat. Flashlights could now be seen coming down into the basin from the road above as officers rushed to the scene.

Officer Waters closed her eyes. The world was shaking. When she opened her eyes, her arms went numb, and the world was falling. Then she hit the ground. Crucified on a blood soaked log, the creature smashed a rock against her head as it attacked her. The giggling of the children filled the air, mixing with the sound of screaming and gunfire. She did not move again.

Moving quickly forward between the trees, Ryan tried to get a better position without being hit by the gunfire coming from the patrol boat. He needed to see whatever this creature was. The creature had disappeared into some heavy brush at the edge of the marsh. The patrol boat had lost sight of the creature and was slowly moving towards the spot it had last been seen.

The first of the backup officers were now slowly moving into the basin, and the sounds of chatter and police radios filled the air. The State Police helicopter was now over the basin, its search-light once again turning the macabre scene into a gray daylight.

Climbing out of the boat, Butch walked quickly over to Ryan as he began to slowly approach, his pistol outstretched before him, where he had seen the creature disappear into the brush. Seeing the ranger moving forward, a few of the officers also started to move toward the place in the underbrush the ranger was pointing to, their guns drawn and ready to fire.

Pushing aside a few of the bushes, Ryan screamed, "Nothing! I saw it go in here, but there's nothing!"

But there was something when they moved forward; Ryan and Hunt knew the creature had been here. Under the glare of lights was the lifeless body of a female police officer, crumpled like a rag doll, broken and bleeding on the ground. Fear was etched on the officer's lifeless face; a gash on her throat and smashed skull were the causes of her death. A bloodied rock nearby and a knife or something sharp had done the job.

"Dear God, its Becky!" one of the officers called out as he stepped through the brush. "What could have done this?" Bending down, he checked her pulse, but he already knew the answer. "She's dead." Standing up, he started to scan the night to find the thing that had killed his fellow officer.

Captain Hunt knew it was too late: the creature again had vanished into the night and back into the Esker. It was now obvious that there was more than one, and they were no closer to catching these things. Glancing around the basin, he could see there were plenty of cops here now.

Chief Smollett was slowly making his way down into the ravine.

"Butch, what the F happed here and on the island!" Pausing for a moment over the dead officer, he began to cry. "I sponsored Becky to join the force. I stood for her when she got married. Now she's dead. Butch, what happened here?"

"Don't know for sure, Bob. What was Becky even doing here?" Hunt looked around, and it seemed everyone was waiting for him to issue some orders or something. "Ryan, take a few men and search down the marsh. Whatever was here must have gone that way. It couldn't have passed us and gone back up into the Esker."

"Got it, Butch. Three of you officers, follow me." Turning, the four men quickly headed into the marsh in search of the creature.

"The rest of you men spread out and secure the area for one hundred yards," Hunt called out to the remaining officers.

"I don't know what that thing was, Bob, but there seems to be more than one, and they're fast and deadly." Hunt knew his old friend had heard him, but the police chief took off his jacket and covered the face of Officer Waters. The blood began to pool and slowly drain toward the salt marshes.

"What do you mean "this thing" and "more than one."? Are you telling me we have a pack of these things running around here on the Esker, killing at will? What makes you think we have more than one?"

"Back in '64, when the McGrath boy and Officer Giannone were killed under the Esker in the storm drains, both rescue teams were attacked at the same time by something only described as being covered in seaweed. Tonight, right after the creature jumped into the Back River, it seems another attack happened here in the basin at that point." Turning toward the basin, Hunt could see a few officers standing over something in the bushes just off to the marsh side of the bonfire.

The grim discovery of three mutilated teens had just been found. "Dear God, what has happened here? Chief Smollett gasped as he walked up to the group of officers. The two boys and one girl were piled on top of the other. It appeared that their skulls had been crushed. "We need to close the Esker and turn over every rock until we find and kill these things."

As he stood over the newly discovered bodies of the three teens, Hunt looked a bit closer. Yes, he knew the three and knew their parents. "I know these kids, Bob."

"Yeah, me too," Smollett replied, bending down to one knee to closer inspect the three bodies. Three kids and three officers killed tonight, and with three missing and most likely dead, it seems we have a deadly problem up here on the Esker."

Moving slowly through the dense underbrush of the Esker and into the tall sea grass of the salt marshes, Ryan kept his gun pointed in front of him as he slowly moved forward. A group of officers followed close behind, their lights showing the way. The smell of the salty marsh was overwhelming to his eyes and senses. After a few minutes of searching the marsh, Ryan knew the creature would not be found tonight.

In the glare of the lights, a storm drain had begun to show as the tide began to retreat from the marshes.

AFTERMATH

TERROR ON THE ESKER! was the lead on all of the local papers the next morning. The town was going nuts demanding answers as to what was happening up on the Esker. Could the creatures come down into the town next? Was it safe to walk the streets? *So many questions and no answers*, Captain Hunt thought while sitting in the small diner at the bottom of Jackson Square. On the local news, Police Chief Smollett sweated these questions with a local news reporter who had trapped him outside his home.

Paul and Ryan sat down at Hunt's table.

It had been a long night and into the morning for the three of them. After the disaster on the Esker, they'd undergone a full four-hour interrogation by special agents of the Massachusetts State Police with a promise of many more in the days to come.

"Morning, Butch. Quite a deadly night," Ryan said. He was sitting next to Hunt, while Paul sat across from the captain. It's not even ten o'clock, and already the news is all over last night and what happened up there on the Esker."

"Well, it's not often something kills three police officers, three teens, with three more missing, all in twenty-four hours. Not to mention there seems to be no clue as to what is that is doing all this," Paul chipped in as he started to drink the coffee the waitress had put in front of him.

"That's not really true, Paul. Let's see, what we do know about this thing?" Hunt asked as he started to write on a pad of paper on the table. "We now know there is more than one. The way things look, it seems that there is a pack of some sort of these creatures up on the Esker."

"Butch, don't you mean under the Esker? Every time we have encountered these things, it has been in the storm drains, or that is where they return to escape from us," the ranger said as he took a long drink of his java.

"Nope. The drains have been searched several times and are being searched again even as we speak. Whatever these creatures are, they just use the drains as passages to get to where they are going without being seen. Chances are, they live off the Esker over by the sand pits or somewhere else that we can find up on the Esker," Hunt said as he continued to write.

"This morning," Ryan said, "I was checking some of the local papers and found some things that have happened on the Esker during the late summer. Pets reported missing and never found, absence of large wildlife. I was told that there was a large population of deer at one point up there." After pausing for a moment, he continued. "Homes near the Esker report trash being dumped and picked through, pets missing from backyards, gardens being pulled apart in the middle of the night. All during late summer months."

"What about the winter and summer months? What happens then?" Paul asked, looking out the window of the small diner.

"Not much. Things on the Esker are pretty quiet during the early summer, and the winters? Forget it; nothing goes on up there."

"It sounds like something is getting ready for the winter months during late summer up there, gathering food for the winter," Hunt said, almost as an afterthought.

"Paul, what are you looking at anyway?" Ryan asked the firefighter.

"I am looking at a food source for the creatures up on the Esker." Outside the window, Paul watched as the herring jumped up the river herring ladders that were there to help them make their journey from the Atlantic Ocean to Whitman's Pond where they mated. "The Herring Run enters in through the Back River, down behind the town dump."

"You're right, Paul, a perfect place to catch fish, as they bunch up there before they make the jump from salt to freshwater. Let's go take a look," Butch said, as he stood and threw a twenty dollar bill on the table.

It was a quick ten-minute walk along side the Herring Run as the men approached the entrance to the run, down behind a local school and close to the town dump. The entrance to the run was a deep inlet where the fresh waters from Whitman Pond mixed in with the saltwater of the Back River. The herring would stay there until they became accustomed to the fresh water and then started their journey up the Herring Run to the pond to mate.

Standing at the edge of the inlet pool, the three men watched as fish swam in slow circles and adjusted to the changes in the water. The process took time, and the fish seemed very easy prey at this time, as every few minutes a large bird would dive towards the water and grab a fish, carrying it away toward the Esker to eat. Some of the bigger predator fish had come in from the deeper waters to eat the easy prey.

"Man, that is a lot of fish," Paul called out as Butch started to walk slowly toward the salt marsh off to the left. It appeared that he'd seen something and was going to check it out. Watching Hunt bend down, Paul asked, "What ya got, Butch?"

"Fish traps, made of sticks and sea grass." Pulling one of the traps out of the water, Hunt could see several fish had already been caught in the wooden trap. "Looks like six traps, all pretty full of fish," called out, dumping the fish out of the trap and back into the slow moving water.

"Pretty crude, but effective fish traps. Do you think our creatures on the Esker are using these to fish here?" Ryan asked as he turned the crude trap over a few times before throwing it back into the water.

"Would seem so. The skill to make something so crude with only sticks and grass would make it a likely bet. But these traps are full, meaning that the creature will be back soon to gather the fish, unless the patrols on the Esker are keeping it from coming down here to collect the fish," Hunt said. Reaching down, he grabbed another trap and emptied the fish out into the water.

"Let's get the cops to post a few men here, and maybe they'll get luckily and catch whatever is setting these fishing traps," Paul said as he emptied another trap full of fish into the water. "I'll wait here, Butch, until the cops show up, and then I'll head back to the station, as I have the afternoon shift."

"Better be careful, Paul. These things seem to be able to hide until it is too late for a person to do anything," Hunt said. He paused for a moment and then continued: "It might be better if you just left with us, Paul." Hunt seemed to know something was again watching the small group of men, just out of sight in the high salt grass marshes that led to the Herring Run from the Back River. "Not sure why, Paul, but I just get a feeling something is watching us from the marshes."

Glancing over to where Hunt was looking, Paul was sure it was just the light morning breeze that was playing tricks in the high grass. "Doubt it, Butch. The way the police have everything buttoned up around here, I doubt anything will be here or anywhere on the Esker. But I think you may be right. Let's head back and call it in and see what the police think."

Turning slowly around, the three men started the short journey back to lower Jackson Square.

"Well, I need to get to the station, as life for the Weymouth Fire Department does go on," Paul called out as he headed across the street to his truck. "See you guys later!"

"Butch, what are you up to today?" Ryan asked, glancing up the square as the slow-moving traffic continued.

"Well, I do have chores at home, and I still need to go down to the boat ramp and get my boat, and there's some yard work to do. And you, what do you have planned for today?"

"Work day, Butch. Got some paperwork to do at the office. Still need to keep the Esker clean and try not to get in the way of the police for the next few days while they finish their job up and hopefully catch this thing up on the Esker."

"Let's hope so, but I doubt it. These things seem to have been around for years without being seen. My only guess is this pack is getting bigger. They need a larger food source and are taking risks and killing anything that gets in their way. Don't forget, Ryan, to tell the police about the Herring Run," Hunt said, he climbed into his truck and pulled into traffic.

Climbing into his truck, Ryan started the short drive to the ranger station at the end of Elva Rd. The traffic was heavy, so he took a right onto East St. to avoid some of the traffic. Police cars, both local and from other towns, were everywhere, driving slowly up one street and down another, all in search of a creature that had killed three of their own. Taking a slow right onto Green St., he could see the local news truck parked on the road, doing a local interview with some of the residents out for a walk. The town of Weymouth was scared, and rightly so; something was killing them.

Pulling his truck into his spot at the ranger station, Ryan could see several local police cars and many state cars, as well as a number of unmarked cars and a large green truck that had brought some of the National Guard to help with the search of the Esker. At least twelve media trucks were scattered about the parking lot, all trying for the best shot of the action and Esker.

"Excuse me. You are the park ranger here, right?" The voice came through the passenger side window of his truck. A microphone followed, thrust close to his face.

"Ah, yes, I am. What can I do to help you? The park is currently closed if you want a tour." Climbing out of his truck, Ryan was sure his answer was not enough to keep the reporter happy.

"Can you explain what is happening on the Esker? With three officers dead in one night, three teens savagely murdered on the same night, local couple hung from a tree and cut up on Whale Island, a missing assistant park ranger who is presumed murdered, and an older couple now confirmed missing and, in all likelihood, dead. All this has happened in just the last few days on the Esker."

"Wait, you said an older couple is missing? How do you know that?" The ranger had now stopped walking, and he turned toward the young news reporter.

"Yes. According to neighbors, Ken and Elisa Keller did not come home yesterday from a late walk on the Esker. Their dog was found badly beaten and dead down by the Boy Scout bridge, covered in trash from a trash can nearby."

"I was not aware that the Kellers were missing, though I did see them yesterday morning on the Esker walking their dog." Turning, Ryan continued into his office.

The chatter was overwhelming as he entered. It seemed every inch of space was occupied by someone. His desk had turned into a map table, as several maps of the Esker were laid across it.

"You're the park ranger, right?" A thick voice called out from across the room. Without waiting for an answer, it continued: "Get over here!"

Ryan walked over to the large man who'd called to him.

"My name is Captain Stan Marsh of the state police special crimes unit." Reaching out, Ryan shook the massive hand outstretched toward him. "I hear you had quite a night up on the Esker. I read your report along with the others. Is there anything you could add?"

"Not really, though we did find some make-shift fishing traps down at the entrance to the Herring Run. Captain Hunt thinks they may have something to do with what is happening up on the Esker."

"Show me on the map where you are talking about and give me a bit more information about it." Marsh pushed the map toward Ryan, and the room became quiet as everyone waited for this new information.

"Well, this morning, Butch, Paul, and I were having breakfast down in lower Jackson Square when we noticed the Herring Run outside. It seems that these things are gathering food for the winter."

"Wait, you said these things are gathering food for the winter? What makes you say that?" someone called out from the group surrounding the table.

"Yes, after a bit of research, it would seem that whatever these things are up on the Esker are gathering food for the winter. Given the fact that there have been multiple attacks at the same time over the years, it is safe to assume that there is more than one, and it appears that the group is growing, forcing them to take more chances to gather food." Stopping for a moment, Ryan could feel the impact of his words on the group of men.

"Anyways, we went to the mouth of the Herring Run, where it meets the Back River, and found several crude fishing traps made out of branches and held together with sea grass. All the traps were full, suggesting they would be emptied soon by someone or something."

"Do we have any units in that area right now? If so, move them to this spot, and if not, let's get a few units down there now. Thanks, Ryan. You can go home now. The Esker will be closed for a few days, and your services as park ranger are not needed at this time. You will be informed when you can resume your duties," the captain said as he made way for Ryan to leave the office.

"Understand something, Captain. These things are not seen until they attack. They appear to be great hunters and blend in very well with the background and go right for the kill. They are not going to be found with a large group. You need to lie in wait for them to appear." Stepping out the door, Ryan stopped for a moment as the news crews started moving forward.

"Can you tell us anything about what is killing on the Esker?" the voices rang out as Ryan pushed past the crowd, climbed into his truck, and drove off.

10,000 YEARS OF ICE

FOR THE NEXT SEVEN days and nights, Great Esker Park was the scene of nonstop police patrols and surveillance. Every storm drain was searched, and every rock was turned. The sound of nervous gunfire filled the air, as sometimes shadows were scarier than nothing at all. At the end of the week, the state police and local officials deemed Esker Park once again safe. People were given advice to only travel in groups during the day and stay on the main road that ran along the top of the Esker. Police would continue to patrol during the day, and the Esker would remain closed at night for the foreseeable future.

Whatever had done the horrendous killings was gone for now, perhaps washed out to sea during a storm or dead at the bottom of the Back River during the gunfight on Whale Island. No one knew for sure. Like with the McGrath child years ago, there were no answers, just more questions.

Pulling his truck into his spot next to the ranger station, Ryan knew that whatever had come to the Esker was still there. Hopefully, it had retired for the winter and would wait until spring before it started again. By that time, he was sure something could be worked out between him, Butch, and Paul to stop this madness from ever happening again.

Walking into his office, he noticed that the place was a mess. The state police had not cleaned it up, but had just left it a mess after they were done. Piles of trash over-flowed from the two trash cans in the office. Boxes of old pizza were piled high on one desk. Half empty coffee cups were everywhere. Every light had been left on, and the bathroom was a mess. Without Kim around, Ryan knew the job of cleaning was left to him. "Man, at least Kim liked to clean," he said to no one as he began to clean his office. "Yeah, Kim liked to clean"

After about an hour of cleaning, a voice called in through the open door: "Hey, Ryan, how is the house work coming?" The voice was familiar to Ryan, but it was a voice from long ago.

"Hey, Todd Fuller, how ya doing?" said Ryan when he realized it was an old high school buddy he had run varsity track with. He stopped his cleaning and walked to the door, stepping out into the bright morning sun. "Good to see you, Todd. How is life treating you these days?"

"Not bad. I heard you were back from Nam and you were the park ranger here on the Esker. Been a tough couple of weeks for you, I bet."

Looking up to the Esker, Ryan knew it had been a tough couple of weeks. Some-how, after all these deaths, there were still no real answers; all were still unsolved. "Hmm, yes, I guess you could say it has been a tough couple of weeks. So, what brings you to the Esker today?"

"Well, I am the cross country coach at the high school and thought I would give my team a bit of hill endurance climbing today. Is that ok with you?"

"I guess so. Just make sure they stay together and don't leave the road. Any problems, tell them to high-tail it back here and let me know."

"Will do, Ryan. All right, men, you heard the ranger. Let's go and stay together. To the drive-in to the dump and back again. Then report back here after the second dump touch. I will get you back on the bus then and back to school for some weights. See you in one hour."

Watching the group of kids run off to the entrance to the Esker, Ryan wanted to believe everything would be alright.

"Well, good seeing you, Ryan. I will be back in an hour to pick them up, let's get together soon and talk about old times." After climbing back into the school van, Todd drove off with a beep of the horn.

"Never really liked that guy, but maybe he has changed," Ryan half said to himself. Turning, he watched the kids clear the ridge of the Esker and start their run to the drive-in a few miles away. "I hope they will be ok."

The Esker was starting to get busy as he watched a few folks start up the trails that led to the road on top. He was not sure if they were thrill seekers or what. In the ranger's mind, the Esker would never be safe until whatever was up there was found and killed. It might be hiding for a bit, but when it got hungry, it would be back on the Esker, stalking prey even if it was human prey.

"Hey, Ryan, what ya thinking about?"

The voice caught Ryan by surprise. It was not often someone could get that close to him without being heard. "Hey, Paul," he replied. "Just watching folks head back to the Esker. Even after the last few weeks, people are willing to risk their lives just in the hope that they can come back with a story to tell."

"I heard from Butch," said Paul. "There are three teams of two police officers patrolling the Esker, so it should be safe for the most part. With the winter approaching, I am thinking things will quiet down until spring."

"Well, you sound almost like you believe that, Paul." Pausing for a moment, Ryan looked at the growing crowd headed to the Esker. News reporters with their cameras struggled up the steep trail to the top. "I don't think this is over. At best, it is over til spring."

"Well, everyone, it seemed, in the world did a thorough search of the Esker, day and night, for a week. Whatever did this is either hiding wicked good, dead, or moved on. Feel like lunch? I am buying," Paul added after a moment.

"Sure, but I have to be back in an hour. After seeing how dirty my office was, I can only image how overflowing the Esker trash cans are. I promised Mrs. Keller I would keep up on that."

"Sure, just an hour it is, then. I am guessing the Chinese buffet up on Bridge St. works for you," Paul said with a grin as he climbed into his truck.

"Haven't been there since before Nam. Got thrown out for being me. I hope they don't remember me." Climbing into the truck, Ryan slammed the door shut.

The lunch took over an hour, as the restaurant was busy. Many of folks there remembered Ryan before and now. Most had questions about what had happened on the Esker. "What was it?" and "Is it safe now?" seemed to be the major questions he fielded all through lunch.

"Hey, Paul, thanks for the lunch," Ryan called out as he climbed out of the truck. "Next time it is on me. My ranger salary is burning a hole in my pocket," He said with a laugh, slamming the door shut.

"Yes, next time you can get the bill. Promise. Well, off to work. Watch yourself up there, Ryan. Give me and Butch a call if you need us." With a wave of his hand, Paul drove off.

Ryan knew he had one job left today, and it was not something he wanted to do. He had not been up on the Esker since that night of terror, and the thought of going back up gave him a few chills. "Well, time to empty the park trash cans. Heck, what could happen? Just don't leave the trail." Besides, the town council had authorized him to carry a weapon. Walking over to his truck, Ryan reached into the glove compartment and pulled out his service weapon, a 1911 Colt forty-five. Strapping the holster to his belt, he checked the weapon to make sure it was loaded and headed to get the mule for the trash run up on the Esker.

Pulling the mule out of the garage, Ryan noticed the van for the high school cross country team had come back. The coach did not seem too happy and appeared to be yelling at the team. Noticing the park ranger, the coach waved him to come over to the bus.

"Hey, Todd, what's up?" Ryan pulled the mule to a halt, shut the noisy vehicle down, and waited for the coach to calm down, as he was still yelling.

"It seems, Ryan, my team can't listen to orders very well. I told them to stay together, and guess what? They didn't!"

"It wasn't our fault, Mr. Todd. Russell does what he always does and just took off from us on the way back the second time from the drive-in."

"Wait, you are saying one of your kids is missing?" Ryan climbed back onto the mule. "Where was the last place you saw him?"

"He was running ahead of us on the hill that leads to the drive-in, coming back from it," one of the kids yelled out from the back of the van.

"Todd, listen. Go inside my office and call Paul at Station One. Tell him what has happened and tell him I am going to look for the boy. He will know what to do. But hurry." Starting the mule, Ryan quickly threw it into gear and started to drive up the Esker in search of the missing youth.

Reaching the top of the Esker, Ryan slowed the vehicle, turned right, and stopped. Climbing off the mule, he grabbed his binoculars and started to scan the marsh area of the Esker. Off in the distance, he could see two people sitting on the beach over at Reversing Falls. "Great, so much for the don't leave the road warning." Continuing to scan the inside of the

Esker, he could see many people had just not paid attention to the road only warning.

"Fantastic! Where are the supposed police patrols that are up here keeping the folks on the road! Something caught his eye, moving just below where he was standing, down in the marsh. "No. it can't be!" the shocked ranger whispered to himself.

The cross country runner had been found. He was sprawled over the storm drain on his back. The same drain Tommy McGrath had entered so many years ago and never returned from. The runner was not moving. Looking quickly around for some help, the ranger knew he needed to get down there to the youth, and he started down the incline.

About halfway down the incline, the ranger stopped, as something had come out of the drain, covered in seaweed and dirt. The creature appeared to be singing as it stood over the youth. Moving closer, Ryan knew that he had found the creature. The problem: what to do about it? Pulling his weapon out, he continued quietly down the steep ravine.

Is the youth dead, or... ran through his mind. The answer came quickly as the youth screamed out in pain "YAAAAA!" The creature had begun cutting into the youth's thigh with what appeared to be a seashell, slicing off a long strip of the fleshly meat. Again, the youth screamed, "Please don't!" Reaching out, the youth tried to push the creature away.

Grabbing the youth by the hair, the creature slammed his head against the concrete drain multiple times.

"Hey, Dumbass! Get away from the kid!" Ryan screamed out as he pointed the weapon at the creature and started to move quickly down the side of the Esker. At that moment, Ryan stopped, as the creature looked up and snarled a menacing, low growl. *Dear God, it is a person.* Lowering his weapon for a moment, it was all the creature needed. Grabbing the youth by the leg, the creature quickly began to pull its prey into the storm drain.

"Stop, stop, stop!" Ryan yelled, moving quickly toward the drain.

The creature was now in the drain and was pulling the screaming youth in after it. The creature was powerful and had pulled the youth into the drain. All that was outside were the youth's hands, holding desperately to the edges of the drain. His screams filled the air as Ryan dove to grab the terrified youth's hand, but he was too late, as the boy lost his grip and was pulled into the darkness of the drain. His hands reaching out in desperation, the boy screamed for help, terror on his face as he disappeared into the deep, endless blackness of the drain, his screams echoing off the concrete walls.

"Dear God!" Ryan called out in desperation. Turning, he quickly began to run to the side of the Esker. Was it fear, or did he need to get help? Maybe a little of both. Half-way up the steep slope, the ground gave way, and he began to fall through the Esker floor into blackness.

"Paul, this is Todd. I am at the ranger station. We have one of my cross country runners missing on the Esker. Ryan went to look for him and told me to call you."

"How long has the kid been missing, Todd?" Paul asked, hoping it was just some kid who'd run home and instead of waiting for the bus. But the pit in his stomach told the firefighter different.

"Couple of hours now, I am guessing. It was just supposed to be a bit of hill running today to get ready for a meet in Milton in a few days. He was told to stay with the group, but he didn't." Todd replied.

Paul thought he seemed to be making excuses for losing a runner.

"Todd, we can assign blame later right now do you have the rest of the track team with you?" he asked as he started to get up from his desk.

"Got the rest of the team in the van, and I am heading back to the high school with them."

"Good. After you drop them off, head back to the Esker and meet me and Captain Hunt there, and we can help Ryan search for the missing kid." After hanging up the phone, Paul started to dial up Butch Hunt, but he did not have to, as he heard Butch enter the station and begin talking to a few of the firefighters in the crew room.

Heading into the crew room, Paul blurted out, "Butch, we have another kid missing on the Esker. Ryan is up there now looking for the kid alone. We need to get up there!" He knew if that creature was around, one person alone did not stand much of a chance in an encounter.

On his back and in pain, Ryan looked up to where he had fallen through. Something or someone was covering the hole in the floor of the Esker. It was a trap, and he had just fallen into it. The ranger's attempts to move were met with great pain. One of his legs was smashed pretty badly from the fall. Reaching down, he could feel the bone sticking out through the skin. Trying to stay focused, he removed his belt and started to tighten it just above his right knee to stop the bleeding.

Something grabbed him by the hair and started to drag him deeper into the pit he had fallen into. Trying to fight back was no use. His leg bumped along, causing great pain. Reaching down to his side, he still had his weapon in its holster, but he would need to wait for a clean shot and a better understanding of where he was and what was attacking him. The painful dragging into. the darkness² continued for what seemed an eternity

The smell of fire and smoke was everywhere as the creature dragged the ranger from the darkness through an opening in the blackness. After a few more feet, the creature let go of the ranger and moved away. Struggling with the pain, Ryan fought to focus his eyes, and he pulled his weapon from its holster. Raising into a sitting position, weapon drawn, Ryan could only say, "What the F…!" as he began to see where the creature had dragged him. It was no creature at all.

It was cold and wet. As Ryan looked around, he could see he was in some sort of cavern. Some of the walls were covered with ice, and the slow steady dripping of it melting could be heard behind him. "Ice of a million years," he said to himself. Yes, he was deep inside the Esker, and what he was looking at had been here for thousands of years.

They were primitive people, a group of thirty or so, covered in animal fur and seaweed. They must have been frozen thousands of years ago as they'd slept. Then they must have started to defrost back in the sixties and picked right up where they'd left off. This cave inside the Esker was their home. The storm drains were the link to the outside.

Off to the ranger's left, he could see a pile of human remains and the boy track runner lying on the ground, still alive. He was crying out in pain as some of the dirty children taunted him by poking sticks at him. They laughed continuously as they tormented to poor kid.

Pulling his weapon, the ranger fired two shots into the air. *Crack! Crack!* The sound of the gun was irresistible in the cave. The kids stopped and started to run to the group of adults, who had turned and started moving toward the ranger. The group seemed to have both men and woman from what the ranger could see as they neared, young and old, and a few seemed to be carrying small children.

"I don't want to hurt anyone!" Ryan screamed out, bringing the gun to bear on the advancing group. "Back off! I am warning you!" he yelled out again as the group moved closer. Ryan opened fire, knocking down the two closest men with clean head shots. But the group was upon him as he shot again. Something hit him in the head from behind, and he blacked out.

"What the F hit me?" Ryan was starting to remember as he tried to move but could not. He was hanging upside down, tied to a post. He tried to move his hands, but they were bound behind him. Looking across the cave, he could see the cross country kid also tied upside down to a post. One of the men was bending down and pointing at the kid tied to the post. A small child who looked about twelve years old stood nearby, watching as the man pointed and grunted at the helpless victim. *Get away from him!"* Ryan screamed out, but it was no use.

After a moment, the man grabbed the teen by the hair and pulled his head back, exposing his neck. With a scream, the man stuck a large sea= shell into the teen's neck and ripped it upward towards his belly, spilling out the teen's insides in one quick motion. The group screamed and yelled, clapping their hands at the work of the man.

With a grunt, the man handed the shell to the child and pointed at Ryan. It was the child's turn to kill its prey. Taking the sea shell, the child slowly walked toward the helpless ranger. It was obvious to Ryan that the father was teaching his son how to clean its prey when caught.

Standing in front of Ryan, the child hesitated for a moment but only for a moment, as the man grunted and pushed the child. Grabbing Ryan by the hair, the child pushed the shell deep into the ranger's throat and began to pull it slowly up into his chest. Ryan tried to yell, tried to scream, but it was no use. As he started to pass out, Ryan watched as his body's insides spilled out of him, crashing to the ground before him. Death came quietly as he blacked out.

"Is it me, or is someone barbequing up here on the Esker?" Amy Sampson asked her husband as they hiked along the trails at the bottom of the marsh. Stopping for a moment, her husband, Dave, sat down on a storm drain pipe the led into the Esker.

"It certainly smells like someone is," Dave said, and he got off the pipe. "Come on, Amy. Let's finish the hike."

As the couple started to walk away, one of the cave people started to climb out of the storm drain.

CPSIA information can be obtained
at www.ICGtesting.com
Printed in the USA
BVHW031726111218
535356BV00001B/75/P

9 781524 654665